THE YEAR WE WERE FAMOUS

by CAROLE ESTBY DAGG

CLARION BOOKS

Houghton Mifflin Harcourt

Boston   New York   2011

CLARION BOOKS
215 Park Avenue South
New York, New York 10003

Clarion Books is an imprint of
Houghton Mifflin Harcourt Publishing Company.

www.hmhbooks.com

LIBRARY OF CONGRESS CATALOGING-IN-PUBLICATION DATA
IS AVAILABLE.

Manufactured in the United States of America

DOC 10 9 8 7 6 5 4 3 2

4500303418

To Clara and Helga

PREFACE

❧⟋∽⟍❧

THE FIRST SEVENTEEN YEARS and three months of my life were so ordinary, they would not be worth the telling. And last May when I came home from high school in Spokane to help Ma, I thought fate had yanked me back to Mica Creek and I would be stuck there on the farm, helping out one more time and one more time until I was buried in the Mica Creek cemetery alongside my brother Henry. I had prayed that I would find a way to get out of Mica Creek. I forgot to stipulate that I would like to get out of Mica Creek without the constant company of my mother and by some means other than my own two feet.

But then, because of Ma, I was briefly famous. Sketches of us appeared in the *New York World* twice: our "before" picture in black silk dresses with leg-o'-mutton sleeves; and our "after" picture in ankle-baring skirts and brandishing guns and daggers. Because of the way our adventure ended, we couldn't talk about it afterward. But I kept my journal. Sometimes, late at night, I would rummage through to the bottom of my hope chest and find my journal. I would read it and remind myself of that life-changing year.

THE YEAR
WE WERE FAMOUS

CHAPTER 1

MICA CREEK

February 28, 1896

I ARRANGED a dozen winter-blooming Johnny-jump-ups in a tall pill bottle and set them on a tray along with three biscuits and coffee in Ma's best teacup. As if it might bite, I took a deep breath and lifted the letter by one corner and laid it across the top of the tray.

I nudged open the door to Ma and Pa's bedroom with my knee. "*God morgen,* Ma! Good morning!" I crossed the room to hold the tray close enough for her to smell hot biscuits and coffee.

Ma groaned and turned to face the wall. "No breakfast. Sleep."

I set the tray on the bedside table and tapped one corner of the envelope against Ma's hand, the one clutching the bedclothes as protection against the real world. "It's another letter from the treasurer. Do you want me to read it to you?"

Ma drew up her knees as if she were making herself a smaller target for bad news.

With the knife from the tray, I slit open the envelope. The treasurer's seal glared out from the top of the letter. It reminded me of the eye of a dead fish. "You are hereby notified that on January 2, 1897, the property in township..."

Eyes still closed, Ma flung her arm to brush the unwelcome words away and instead bumped the tray, spilling the coffee and soaking the biscuits. She covered her ears.

"Ma, you have to listen!"

As if in league with my intent to rouse Ma from bed today, Marmee jumped on the bed to lick Ma's cheek and purr into her ear. Ma swiped Marmee's paw away from her face.

I lifted the cat off the bed so I'd have a place to sit. "Refusing to listen to this letter isn't going to make it disappear. Since Pa doesn't read English, he leaves all the business to you, and we are a sheriff's auction away from losing this house and everything in it."

Ma still played possum, so I crossed the room and jerked the window shade cord, letting the shade snap to the top, and opened the window as far as it would go.

She turned her back to the light and pulled the quilt over her head. "Cold," she said.

"Refreshing," I countered.

She forced a cough. "I can't get up," she said. "I have consumption."

"Half of Mica Creek has a cough this winter, Ma. I don't

think it's consumption. And even if it is, fresh air and exercise are the best things for it."

"And it's not just consumption. You don't understand what it's like to have a sensitive spirit."

I pictured Henry in his coffin: eleven years old, hands gnarled like an old man's by the childhood arthritis that had spread through his body and stopped his heart. "We all miss Henry," I said, smoothing the coverlet over Ma's shoulder, "but keeping busy is the best cure for sadness. You have to get out of bed sometime. Are you going to wait until the farm is auctioned off and Pa carries you off on the mattress?"

Ma burrowed deeper into the covers. So much for rousing her today.

I carried the puddled tray with soggy biscuits back to the kitchen so I could get on with the rest of my chores—more accurately, Ma's chores, which she had been leaving to me for the last two months. But first I'd drink what was left in her cup. She always said coffee would stunt my growth, but I didn't care. I was already taller than half the boys my age.

Three loaves of bread dough had risen an inch above the rim of their pans; while they baked, I'd scrub the sink and the table, spot clean the floor, and refill the wood box. By the time everyone else was out of bed and had run through their chores, the bread would be ready.

Hot air from the oven flushed my cheeks as I slid the first two pans into the wood stove. Making room for the third pan, I burned my knuckles.

"*Uff da!*" I let the oven door slam and blew on my hand as I crossed the room to put the backs of my burned fingers against the ice in the corner of the window. The heat of my fingers melted through the frost. Past the orchard, dormant wheat fields were tucked under six inches of powdery snow. I felt like the winter wheat, holed up and hibernating, waiting for my time to sprout. If you planted wheat, you got wheat, but what was I meant to grow into?

I splayed the palm of my good hand against the frost on the window. I was seventeen years old, but lye soap and kitchen, laundry, and garden chores had given me the hands of a forty-year-old. Piece by piece my parents' farm in Mica Creek was turning me into someone I did not want to be.

I scratched my initial in the thinning ice toward the middle of the pane. *C* for Clara. *C* for *clever*? Clever enough to stay at the top of my high school classes, even while working at least twenty hours a week for my room and board in Spokane, but not clever enough to think of a way to save the farm. Ice collected under my fingernail as I sketched a kindergarten-style oblong house on the window, then huffed on the frost and wiped it out.

I looked back at the kitchen: the water pump handle where our hands had worn off the red paint; the marks on the door frame where Marmee scratched to be let out; our heights recorded each year on our birthdays on the wall next to Ma and Pa's bedroom... If we didn't get money soon, we'd have to leave it all behind. Even though I wanted to leave Mica Creek and go away to college, I had always assumed this house would be here forever, to come back to.

It was quiet...all I could hear was the ticking of the regulator clock. Time was running out.

CHAPTER 2

SPRING CLEANING

March 15, 1896

4:30 a.m.

WHEN I heard the thunks of something heavy hitting each plank of the back porch steps, I wiped my floury hands on my apron and dashed toward the door just in time to open it for Ma. She was lugging in the stepladder from the barn. Since she had not stirred from bed for nearly three months, I was amazed to see her not only up, but dressed and apparently ready to start some project that involved a ladder. But that was Ma—weighted down in misery for weeks and then, with no preamble, up and bustling again.

"What are you doing up so early, Ma?"

Ma grinned. "Spring cleaning! Just look at that soot on the ceiling above the wood stove."

"I know it's dirty, but why don't we wait until everyone's had breakfast and the kids are off to school?"

"If you wait for the perfect time to clean, it doesn't get done; you just have to jump in and do it."

"You're a fine one to lecture after spending months in bed," I said. As Ma raised her eyebrows, I reached out for a hug. "Never mind," I said. "I'm glad to see you up. Truly."

"Well then. Let's fill the kettle and get going."

Pa shuffled out of the bedroom, rubbing his eyes. "I thought I heard you up, Mrs. Estby!" His eyes glowed with a tenderness that made me blush. I hoped someone besides Erick Iverson looked at me that way someday.

After Pa went to the barn for milking, I pumped water into the copper wash kettle and lugged it to the wood stove. Between batches of biscuits, I refilled Ma's buckets and wiped up her spills. She had moved the ladder several times and scrubbed half the ceiling before the kids started trailing downstairs for breakfast.

As usual, the boys were first. Olaf, Johnny, Arthur, and William clomped slowly down the stairs until they saw Ma; then they rushed to be first for a hug. Johnny slipped on water that had dripped down from the ceiling, and stumbled into the ladder. In a flying leap, I caught the ladder in time to save Ma from a fall, but the pail balanced on the top of the ladder slid off, dumping dirty scrub water on the floor — and me. William and Arthur started to laugh, but smothered their chuckles when I gave them my sternest big-sister glare.

I was still wringing out my apron at the sink when Ida entered the kitchen carrying baby Lillian. Bertha lagged several steps behind her. "Ma's up?" she said, as if she could scarcely credit the evidence of her own eyes.

"Ma's up!" the boys chorused. Once they had certified that fact, they surrounded me to ask what we were having for breakfast.

"No sit-down breakfast this morning," I snapped. "There are biscuits and I'll boil eggs." Marmee attempted figure eights around my shins as I took the pot to the pump for water, then went back to the stove, found eggs in the larder, and slid each into the water to boil.

Fifteen minutes later, Ida set to buttering biscuits and peeling eggs. Everyone stood around eating and dropping crumbs and morsels of egg yolk on the floor.

I sliced bread and cheese for lunches and lined up lunch pails. Ma gave each child another hug as he or she went out the door to cross the orchard toward the school. I sent William and Marmee back to the barn with Pa and set Lillian up with canning jar lids and a basket of spools in Ma's room, leaving the door open so I could keep an eye on her.

I offered to take over on the ceiling, but Ma said she liked seeing how much difference she was making. She sang and hummed as she cleaned. There wasn't a tidy way to wash a ceiling, but Ma's exuberant flourishes with the cleaning rags sent even more water dripping down the walls and onto the floor than usual. I followed behind, mopping up.

"I wish you'd worry more about saving the farm than cleaning soot off the ceiling. We won't have a ceiling to wash if we don't pay off our back taxes and mortgage."

"I can do more than one thing at once," Ma said, wringing out another cleaning rag and splashing more water on the floor.

"So what ideas are you coming up with?" I said.

"Well..."

From the length of time she stalled, I wasn't sure she'd been thinking about our debts at all until I prodded her.

She looked down from the ladder. "They're still finding gold in Colorado. I couldn't get Pa to go two years ago, but maybe he would go now that we have to come up with money quickly."

"I think most of the good mining sites are already taken, Ma."

"Or how about drilling for oil again? I'm sure it's there somewhere; those wildcatters just didn't know where to drill."

"The rest of Mica Creek is still laughing about that one, Ma." The skeleton of a rig still stood on the northeast corner of our wheat fields and a pair of hawks surveyed their territory from its height.

"If you don't like my ideas, come up with your own, then." Ma got down long enough to move the ladder and get a fresh pail of hot water.

I had been thinking for months, but all my ideas were as

fanciful or worthless as Ma's. Pa's back still pained him from when he fell off a roof carpentering in Spokane, so he wouldn't be earning much between now and next January. Most women didn't get paid more than a dollar a day with factory work, washing clothes, or even teaching. We needed more than a thousand dollars.

As Ma climbed the ladder with her bucket, she said, "Jenny Lind sang her way across two continents and probably earned five dollars every time she opened her mouth."

"Do you think anyone would pay to hear us sing? They wouldn't even let us in the choir." Mica Creek Lutheran had put out a call for new members after their first soprano, Maija Bagnold, died, but they hadn't been desperate enough to take us. My voice wasn't any better than Ma's, but at least my ear was keen enough to know we were always at least a quarter tone off true.

Ma started scrubbing at a stubborn sooty spot above the stove. She looked down as she wrung out her rag again. "How about shooting, like Annie Oakley in Buffalo Bill's Wild West show? I could make the costumes and you could do the shooting." I looked up from mopping the drips on the floor in time to catch Ma's grin. This time she flicked a few drops of water down at me on purpose.

I wiped my face with one sleeve. "I'm sure your costumes would be spectacular, but you know I can't hit the broad side of a hay wagon at five paces. Be serious—we have to come up with something."

"We have months to think of something. It'll come to us. How about writing? It can't be that hard to write a book. Whenever you can't think of the right word you can look in *Roget's Thesaurus*, and you have an editor to correct your commas and spelling."

Just one book like *Little Women* or *Black Beauty* would pay our bills, but writing was just as ridiculous a suggestion as finding gold in Colorado or learning to shoot as well as Annie Oakley. I still winced to remember what my freshman English teacher had written across the top of my first story: "Good spelling. Lacks poetic imagination." When the books I wrote someday sold thousands of copies, I'd prove that teacher wrong, but I couldn't learn enough about writing in time to do any good.

Ma filled the silence with more singing as she scrubbed. Periodically, Lilly would come into the kitchen to check on us, and I'd find something else to amuse her, like Ma's button jar or the box of alphabet blocks Pa had made that had passed to each child in turn.

We took a break at noon when Pa came in with Billy, but the two of them went back out to the barn as soon as they had eaten. If he kept on polishing the tines on the cultivator they'd be worn down to stubs before spring. After Ma put Lilly down for a nap on the big bed in her room, we were ready to scrub again.

When she had finished the ceiling, she pulled every pot, pan, and bowl out of the Hoosier cabinet and stacked them on the table so she could empty the flour and sugar bins into them. In the process, fine flour dust settled onto the damp floor, turning to paste. I continued following along behind her, sweeping and wiping down. We sometimes called these Ma's whirlwind moods, and for good reason.

When the kitchen door opened again, I didn't look up until I heard Erick's voice. "*Hei,* Mrs. Estby...Clara," he said.

I bolted up from my hands and knees where I'd been scrubbing soot and floury goo from around the legs of the wood stove. "*Hei,* Erick." I flushed—from embarrassment as well as exertion. My apron was damp and smudged in a band at knee-level from kneeling on a wet floor, the cuffs of my chore dress were sopping with scrub water, and the constant steam from the copper kettle had put a sheen of perspiration on my face and plastered loose strands of hair to my forehead and cheeks. Even my best was not very good, and I was not at my best.

Erick swiped off his cap. "I did knock," he said.

Ma wiped her hands on her apron. "I guess we were making too much racket with our pots and pails to hear it. Come on in."

Erick closed the door behind him. "I came over to see if I could help with anything and found Mr. Estby in the barn. He said you were up today, Mrs. Estby, and I thought I'd drop in and tell you how happy we all are to hear it. You've all been through some rough times..." Here he paused, fixing me with a lambent gaze.

"Clara, excuse my rudeness," he said, "but did you know your whole face is covered with flour?" He reached one finger toward my cheek, as if to write his name there, and I drew back.

"Sorry," he said as he looked at the flour bins draining by the sink, at the ladder, and back to me. "Well, I can see this isn't the time for a social call." He nodded toward Ma. "I'll be sure to tell my mother that you've got your starch back."

"You tell your mother *hei* for me, and I'll see you all at church," Ma said.

As soon as Erick backed out of the door, Ma returned to scrubbing down the Hoosier cabinet. "That Erick, there's a catch for you," Ma said.

"I wouldn't want a man I had to catch," I said.

"If you were chasing him, I don't think Erick would run very fast," Ma said.

I went to the sink to wash my face and scrub the stains from my cuffs. I had known Erick since I was ten, when we moved from the sod house in Minnesota to the farm next to his family's place. When we met, Erick answered my smile with a grin that showed off those perfect teeth of his. "I think I'll call you Rabbit," he said. Ever since then I had smiled with my mouth shut.

Ma still hummed while she worked, but she was so far off-key that the tune was hard to identify. I finally made a guess—more by rhythm than by the melody. "Is that 'Nelly Bly'?"

Ma acted offended that I had to ask. "Can't you tell?" she said, and started singing the words:

Nelly Bly! Nelly Bly! Bring the broom along.
We'll sweep the kitchen clean, my dear,
And have a little song.

"I wish I could be like the real Nellie Bly," I said. "Imagine the *New York World* paying her to go clear around the world." Nellie Bly had started her trek two weeks before my eleventh birthday in 1889 and finished seventy-two days, six hours, eleven minutes, and fourteen seconds later in January 1890. I'd kept a scrapbook of all the articles she wrote and even cut my bangs—which I still wore—to look more like her.

"Nellie Bly had it easy," Ma said. "She had a special train take her from New Jersey to California, and the newspapers bought her tickets for ships across the Pacific and Atlantic."

She put down her cleaning cloth and stared out the window, as if seeing something besides the orchard and the wheat fields. "What if a woman—without any help—walked on her own two feet clear across the country? Do you suppose the *New York World* would pay me to do that?"

"Anyone can walk," she said. Her face glowed, and not just from the late-afternoon sun streaming through the kitchen window. "But what if I walked farther than any woman has walked alone before? I'm going to write the *New York World* and see if they will pay me to do it, like they did Nellie Bly."

A month ago, Ma could hardly make it from her bed to the outhouse without me wrapping one arm around her waist to support her. How could she hope to walk clear across the country?

She sighed when she saw my dubious expression. "I know, it won't be that simple. But I have to try something, don't I?"

Ma pulled me down to a chair and kneeled before me. "We cannot lose this farm, Clara. With land, you can grow your own food and have your own hens and milk cow. We're poor here, but at least we eat."

"You don't need to tell me that, Ma. I know."

Ma was finally facing facts, but walking across the country wasn't the most sensible way to raise money. The fire in Ma's eyes was so hot, I had to look away for a moment before I spoke. "I suppose you mean for me to stay home another year while you tromp off across the country," I said.

"I'd be walking for you as well as the farm," she said. "If I come back with a satchel full of money, you won't have to work your way through college. You can just sit under the maple trees and discuss Shakespeare and the meaning of life…" Ma's voice trailed off. Her unfocused eyes seemed to be looking back to a past that did not include getting married at fifteen.

"How long do you think you'd be gone?" I said. Even my bones felt limp.

Ma looked at the clean ceiling, her lips moving in silent calculation. "Six or seven months. I'd be home well before Christmas."

"Won't Pa — won't everyone — say your place is here, Ma? With your family? If someone makes the walk, shouldn't it be me?"

Ma ran her hand gently along my arm. "Clara, you're a good daughter, but you're not much of a showman. To generate enough hoopla to make it worth someone's money, I'll have to talk up the trip with every newspaper reporter between Mica Creek and New York City. Maybe meet governors and mayors as I pass through. This enterprise is not a project for a hide-your-light-under-a-bushel person."

Ma was right. Just the thought of talking to all those strangers made me itch. I didn't want to look at Ma. If she really did go on her walk, I would be stuck here in Mica Creek for the best part of another year, taking over for her. Again.

CHAPTER 3

MA WRITES LETTERS

March 20, 1896

I WAS as jumpy as a colt smelling cougar scat. It was clear that walking across the country wasn't just a daydream; Ma was putting her daydream into action. She started by writing letters. Letters to her Spokane suffrage friends, companies in New York, railroads, and governors of every state from Washington to New York. She even wrote to William Jennings Bryan and William McKinley, who were both running for president. She spent all her egg money on stamps and stationery, and Pa was so relieved to have her out of bed that he humored her by taking her letters to the post office, seven miles away in Rockford.

One night after the other children were in bed and I'd just finished cleaning up the kitchen, I overheard Ma and Pa discussing something in their bedroom. I could tell from the inflections that they were arguing—but about what? In the shadow of the wood stove, I held my breath and pricked my ears.

"Nei," Pa said. *"Nei."* Pa was lean, but he was not light on his feet. Even without his boots on, each footstep connected with the floor in a solid thump as he crossed the bedroom.

I crept toward the door.

"Ja," Ma said. "It's the only way to save the farm."

My heart fluttered. Had she found someone to sponsor her walk? She wouldn't go if Pa firmly forbade it, though. Would she? I slid cautiously toward the door.

"If we're meant to have the farm, we'll have it," Pa said. "You shouldn't risk your life tromping clear across the country on this stunt."

"God gave us brains and expects us to use them instead of just wringing our hands and saying if it's meant to be, it will be. Besides, it's not a stunt; it's a mission, Mr. Estby." I could picture Ma crossing her arms in front of her chest and setting her mouth in a determined line.

"How about Lilly," Pa said. "She's still a baby. And William and Johnny and Bertha...they need their mother even more than they need the farm."

"We can't let the farm go after all the work we've put into it." Now it was Ma's footsteps I heard crisscrossing the room. Her pacing halted and she spoke again. "And this house! You put every nail in it yourself. How could you bear to let anyone else live in it?"

"But you've been in bed with consumption for months," Pa said. "You can't possibly make it across the country. I wouldn't sleep the whole time you were gone for worrying about you." Pa paused. "I'd rather lose the farm than my wife."

"Fresh air and exercise are the best cures for consumption," Ma said. "I can take care of myself."

I doubted it. She was thirty-five years old and had borne ten children, counting the one who died as a baby and Henry. She might have prodigious energy today, but that usually didn't last. She didn't have the stamina to walk day after day clear to New York. If anyone went, it should be me.

I was listening so intently for what Pa said next, and thinking of more reasons I should walk instead of Ma, that I jumped when something touched my leg. It was Marmee, wanting to be let out. I picked her up to keep her from meowing. "Just a minute," I whispered.

"What if you get hurt in the middle of nowhere and there's no one to help?" Pa went on. "You could die in the middle of the plains and I wouldn't even know where to look for your body."

"I'll follow the railroad lines so I'll never be far from help, and I'll leave a clear trail by checking in at every newspaper office I pass. I'll make you a copy of the map I mean to follow."

Pa sighed. "Maybe Olaf could go with you."

"I can't take a man with me. That's the whole point—that a woman can make it clear across the country on her own, without a man's help."

Unfortunately that was the last thing I got to hear. Some of the pesky hairs Marmee had shed on my face found their way into my nose. I snorted gently, then dropped the cat and pinched my nose to muffle the sneeze. *Uff da!*

The voices stopped and Ma flung open the bedroom door. "*Fi da,* Clara! Why aren't you in bed by now?"

"Marmee wanted out," I said. It was the truth, at least partly.

Ma glanced around the room, as if looking for Marmee to confirm my excuse. The cat was waiting by the door. "*Ja,* well. Let her out. Then off to bed." She put her hands on her hips to show she meant what she said, and watched to make sure I went all the way up the stairs. I did go to the bedroom, but I didn't sleep. Would Pa talk her out of the trip? If Pa won the argument, it would be a first. After a point he didn't argue, but he still often got his way in the manner a dog herds sheep: by blocking every direction a sheep takes until it has no choice but to go the way the dog wants it to.

As soon as I heard Pa get up the next morning, I slipped to the kitchen barefoot to start the fire and boil Pa's coffee. By the time he was back from the barn, I had a cup waiting for him.

Pa had been nearly twice Ma's age when they married; he looked even older this morning. His thinning hair was all cowlicks, and the creases at the edges of his pale blue eyes had deepened overnight. The thin, straight nose and elegant cheekbones Ida and Bertha had been fortunate enough to inherit now made him look wan and pinched.

Glancing toward the bedroom where Ma was still asleep, I half whispered. "Pa, you aren't going to let Ma go, are you?"

Pa put both elbows on the table and cradled his cup in his hands. He bent his head to take a sip. "You don't know your Ma if you think I can talk her out of anything she has her mind set on. She's found someone to take her up on this walking idea, and she's so hepped up on this notion that nothing short of tethering her to the bedpost would keep her home."

"I'm sorry, Pa. This whole thing is partly my fault. We were trying to think of ways to save the farm and I started mooning about wanting to be like Nellie Bly and seeing the world, and that sparked her idea of walking across the country."

"So you'd like to be like Nellie Bly?"

"I'd never be crazy enough to walk clear across the country by myself." I meant what I said when I said it, but just the words triggered daydreams of writing stories as I went from town to town, and of people from coast to coast reading about my adventures.

Pa tilted his head quizzically, and I regained my common sense.

"Of course I wouldn't do it, and Ma shouldn't try it, either," I said. "She could break a leg."

"I know." Pa bent his head for another sip.

"She could have another of her dismal spells, and she'd have no one with her who understood her and her moods."

"I know." Pa sighed.

I wondered if Ma would get to see the site of the Chicago

World's Fair, if she'd meet Indians, or see buffalo on the Great Plains. My head was so far away from the kitchen in Mica Creek that I missed what Pa said next. "I'm sorry—what?"

Pa leaned forward, glancing at the bedroom door to make sure Ma wasn't up yet. "I said, since I can't talk Ma out of it, would you be willing to go with her?"

Maybe when I'd said she shouldn't be so far from home without someone to help her he thought I had been hinting that I should go with her. I had fantasized about traveling across the country before, but I had never imagined walking every step of the way with Ma. It was Ma as well as Mica Creek that I wanted to get away from while I figured out my life. And I knew the difference between fantasies and real life. In fantasies, your heart thrilled to feel the ground shake at the thunder of a hundred wild horses. In real life, your heart, lungs, and everything else got mashed as a hundred stampeding horses spooked and trampled you. Walking the twenty-five miles home, as I had on long weekends when I attended high school in Spokane, took nearly all day, but then I could tend my blisters and rest. To get from here to New York, I'd have to get up, blisters or no, and walk twenty-five miles again the next day, and the next day, and the next... "For seven months?"

"I doubt that you'll be gone seven months. You know how she gets with her notions. She will probably burn out before she gets to Walla Walla and you'll both be back before harvest. I just want to have someone with her, to make sure she gets back home."

"Who would take care of Billy and Lilly and all of the others if both of us go?"

"Ida's old enough to look after them."

"She's only fourteen," I said.

"You were only twelve when Ma broke her pelvis and you took over for her."

The blood pounded at my temples. I wasn't a flibbertigibbet who could blithely agree to walk across the whole country like it was just tripping over to the next farm. And I wasn't crazy. I knew this walk would be harder than Ma expected. Could Ma hold on to the energy she had now for seven months?

Pa said, "If you're worried about Erick, I don't think you need to be. He'll still be waiting for you when you get back." He smiled reassuringly.

"Pa, I know you like Erick, and I like him, too. But I don't want to get married—not now. I want to see more of the world."

"Here's your chance then!" Pa looked at me expectantly.

I closed my eyes.

"Yes or no, Clara. Stop mugwumping and get off the fence."

I restrained my half smile as I thought of what the girls at Lewis and Clark High School would think when they found out I was walking all the way to New York City. I had been Cinderella Clara, the one who had to hire out as a domestic to have a place to live while I went to school. I had been the skittery country mouse, too timid to look anyone in the eye. If I went with Ma, I might become famous, right along with her.

This would be my year abroad, my year to turn the old Clara into someone bold, someone with newfound talents, strengths, and purpose in life. Those uppity girls from Lewis and Clark would read about me in the papers and say, "Oh, yes! I knew Clara Estby from school. She was a quiet one, but deep. I always knew she'd surprise us someday."

I opened my eyes and did not restrain my smile. *"Ja,"* I said, "if you think I should."

When we heard Ma's rustling from the bedroom, Pa and I looked toward the door.

He smiled; at least I think he did. His bushy, reddish-brown mustache all but covered up his mouth. "You're a good girl, Clara," he said. "I know it's asking a lot, dealing with Ma by yourself away from home. I doubt if you'll really have to go the whole way."

He raised his cup toward me in thanks. *"Tak,"* he said. "Pretend to be surprised when Ma asks you to go with her."

My mouth gaped open as I watched Pa go back out to the barn. What had I gotten myself into?

A week later, when Ma received a letter from New York, I found out.

Note to Mrs. Helga Estby: Per your instructions, I have added 'and her daughter' to Clause 2. Miss A. J. Waterson

Contract between Waterson Press and Mrs. H. Estby

1. The walk from Washington State to New York City shall be completed by November 30, 1896, although by mutual agree-

ment this time may be extended in case of unpreventable delays
such as illness.

2. Mrs. Estby and her daughter will start their trip with no
more than $5.00 apiece and they must earn additional money
as needed for food, lodging, and replacing shoes and clothing.

3. Mrs. Estby must document her trip by granting interviews
and obtaining signatures of governors, mayors, or other notables
along her route. She must also submit monthly logs of miles
walked.

4. Mrs. Estby will not divulge the name of the party with whom
she has made this contract, who wishes to remain anonymous
until Mrs. Estby has completed the book based on her travels and
it is published.

In return for meeting all these conditions, I, A. J. Waterson, will
award to Helga Estby the sum of $10,000 as an advance
against the proceeds of lecture fees and the sale of her book.

Signed _____   Signed _____
A. J. Waterson, Editor   Helga Estby (Mrs. Ole Estby)

Date _____   Date _____

CHAPTER 4

PACKING UP

"WHO is Miss A. J. Waterson?" I asked, poking one finger at her signature. "I've never heard of Waterson Press."

Ma shrugged and averted her eyes from mine. "Well, I don't know Miss Waterson personally, of course. But one of my suffrage society friends suggested a New York publisher. You just have to let enough people know what you want, and someone will know someone who can help you. That's part of hoopla — something you could use a little more of yourself."

I was too distracted to take offense at Ma's criticism. My hands holding the contract trembled; my heart forgot to beat. We were really going to do it.

In a whirlwind of activity, Ma took care of the hoopla and I took care of the details. She talked the husband of another of

her Spokane friends into taking our picture so we'd have copies to send to the newspapers and sell along the way. She also
talked him into printing two hundred postcard-size calling cards,
or—as she airily called them—*cartes de visite*. They read:

Mrs. H. Estby and daughter,
Pedestrians. Spokane to New York.

I didn't rate my own name on the cards.

She sent a copy of our photograph to the *New York World,*
along with a letter explaining her desperation to save the farm
and her passionate support of women's suffrage. A week later, she
received a large envelope in reply. The editor had ignored Ma's
letter entirely. His article made us sound like two adventuresses
out on a foolish lark:

> Mrs. H. Estby and her daughter of Spokane, Washington,
> have announced their intention to walk from that distant
> city to New York. They expect to break all records in the
> line of pedestrianism and will travel rapidly, with very
> light equipment. They intend to write up their adventures
> afterwards if they survive the experiment.
>
> —*New York World* Sunday Magazine,
> April 26, 1896, page 24

Ma convinced the mayor of Spokane to write us a letter
of introduction on official city stationery so everyone along the
way would know we were respectable women they could safely
welcome into their homes. When we gave our interview for the

Spokane Chronicle, I got the impression that the reporter thought we wouldn't last to the Washington-Oregon border.

Ma said she'd thought of everything, but she missed a few details, like where the five dollars apiece start-up money was going to come from and how we were going to outfit ourselves for the walk. She must have guessed I had a secret college fund. It had taken me four years, taking in ironing at nine cents an hour, to earn that money. It took Ma one trip to the general store in Rockford to spend it. We came home with new work boots for me, two canteens, first-aid supplies, two tins of matches, two oilskin ponchos, a tin of tooth powder and two toothbrushes, two journals and six pencils, and a secondhand satchel a little smaller than a doctor's bag, with a sturdy leather bottom and waxed canvas sides.

We planned to leave in early May, well past any chance of snow in the mountain passes we would have to cross in Oregon. The day before we set out, Erick walked me up to the little rise in the land between his family's farm and ours. Perhaps he did have a little poetry in his soul, because he stood silently on the hill, waiting for the top rim of the sun to disappear behind the horizon before he spoke. He grinned and smoothed his hair, which he had plastered down with pomade this evening instead of leaving it loose across his forehead. He opened his mouth as if to speak, then closed it, while a blush that rivaled the pink of the sunset spread across his cheeks. His right hand fumbled with something in his pocket. Was this the moment he would ask *The Question I Didn't Want to Answer*?

"I wonder how many bushels an acre you'll get this year," I said, bending down to pick a stalk of wheat.

Erick touched my shoulder. "Come on, Clara—I don't want to talk about grain right now. Not with you leaving tomorrow. I have something I want to give you."

If I had to marry someone and live in Mica Creek for the rest of my life, Erick would be the one I'd choose. He was kind and hard-working and nobody in the county knew more about wheat. Kids—and the ladies—liked him; men respected him, although he was only twenty.

But why did he court me instead of my younger sister Ida? Her hair was such a pale blond, it was almost silver. Mine was the color of old hay, or, more charitably, like the light brown flecks on a tweedy sparrow. Her nose was straight and finely molded. The nicest word for my nose was *snub*. Ida made folks laugh, organized hay rides, and decorated the grange for dances. I guessed Erick liked me for the same reason he liked his horse: we were both strong and reliable.

His hand was out of his pocket, and in that hand was a three-inch square plain cardboard box. "I almost got you a ring, but you're such a sensible girl, I knew you'd rather I spent the money on something practical."

I was relieved that it wasn't a ring, but what else would fit in that box?

He turned it over so I could read the lettering: "Magnetic Pocket Compass, Keuffel and Esser, New York."

"They make the best compasses in the country," he said. "And I wanted you to have the best, when you're going so far from home."

I took off the lid and slid the compass from its thin cloth pouch while Erick held open the box.

"Genuine nickel silver, with a lid you open like a pocket watch, so you don't break the beveled glass top. It has this little thingbobby you can thread a cord through, so you don't lose it." His hand brushed mine as he pointed out the features. "Do you know how to use one? See, you hold it flat in your palm and turn the compass needle — see the red end? That's the end that points north. Turn the compass housing — that's this big part — until the big N for *north* lines up with the red needle."

He tried to show me how to use the direction needle, too, but I was so giddy — partly from relief he hadn't outright asked me *The Question*, and partly nervy over thinking about leaving tomorrow — that I just shook my head.

"That's all right. Girls don't really have a head for gadgets; just remember that red points north."

I'd normally have set him straight about what a mere girl was capable of, but this wasn't the time for it. Who knew how much money he had spent on this compass, and his intent was generous. "Thank you," I said. "I'm sure it will prove useful."

I truly regretted that I didn't love him.

Responding to the sadness that must have crept into my face, he said, "I know, it's sad to leave home. But it's another sign of your good character that you were willing to go, to take care of your ma."

Avoiding Erick's gaze, I ran one finger around the rim of the compass case.

"When you look at that compass, I hope you'll think of me. I wanted to make sure you could find your way home to us — to me."

He gently took the compass from my hands, refitted it into its pouch and box, and gave it back to me to put into my pocket. Capturing my hands in his, he fixed his moony blue eyes on my not-so-moony speckled ones. "We can get married after next harvest, when you and your ma get back," he said.

He didn't ask; he took it for granted that we would marry. The only question in his mind was when.

I gently withdrew my hands from his and turned, pretending to be enthralled by the traces of pink and gold fading into the horizon. When I turned back, he was grinning so earnestly that I felt sorry for him. No doubt he thought the tears that welled in my eyes were from happiness.

"Could I give you my answer when I get back from New York?" I wiped my face with the back of my hand and forced a smile. "That is, if Ida hasn't snapped you up by then."

Erick stepped forward and brushed one last damp spot on my cheek. The pad on his finger was callused, but his touch was as gentle as the breath of a kitten. "It's not your sister Ida I'm asking. It's you."

The last morning at home was a blur. The only one of my brothers and sisters who didn't offer last-minute advice or caution was baby Lillian—unless you counted clutching my skirts and whimpering as advice to stay at home.

Pa had loaned me his pistol. I felt the heft of it cradled in my two hands; remembered the jolt of the recoil the first time I shot it last week, practicing with Pa and Arthur. *Ma and I are really going to do this,* I thought. Tomorrow Ma and I would be taking off on a journey of nearly four thousand miles with a .32-caliber five-shot self-cocking pistol. I hoped I'd never have to use it.

Besides what we'd bought in Rockford, Ma had packed the pictures and *cartes de visite* she'd had printed; Mayor Belt's letter of recommendation; a copy of the *New York World* article; maps; a few things from home like a washcloth and soap; a curling iron; and a pepper gun she had made out of an insect sprayer, following directions from one of her suffragist friends. She also had Pa's pocket watch, which she'd threaded on a cord to wear under her shirtwaist. I wore Erick's compass.

Just before we left, we gathered in the kitchen. For the first time since I'd reached my grown-up height, Pa wrapped me in a bear hug. His mustache scratched my cheek, and I breathed in the familiar smell of him: soap from washing up, harness leather, sawdust, hay, and eastern Washington soil.

"Love you, Pa," I whispered.

After Pa let me loose, he took my hand and pressed something into it. "Bring her home if this walk gets too hard."

I opened my hand. Nestled in my palm lay an owl, an inch high, carved of cherry wood and burnished as smooth as a mirror. Pa hadn't carved feathers, a beak, or eyes. Just the wise soul of an owl as a reminder of his trust in me to bring Ma safely back to him.

"I will," I promised. And if highwaymen, cougars, or stampeding cattle didn't finish me off first, it was a promise I would keep.

Lillian sensed that this was no ordinary leave-taking. She plucked at Ma's shoelaces, sobbing, "Off, off!" Pa picked Lillian up so Ma could hug her one last time. Ma's eyes glistened, but I couldn't tell if it was from second thoughts or pure excitement.

Pa's voice was husky as he said goodbye.

Ma gave each child one last hug and turned to go. By the kitchen door hung a gilded picture of an angel. As we left the house for the last time, Ma kissed her fingers and pressed them to the angel's heart. I did the same.

Forty paces down the path to the main road, I turned and looked back. My sisters and brothers had started back toward the house, but Pa was still standing at the gate by Ma's Austrian Copper rose. One strap of his overalls had slipped halfway down his shoulder, and he clutched his hat in both hands over his heart. The whole scene blurred for a moment until I blinked. When he raised his hand to wave, I caught up to Ma and touched her sleeve.

"Pa's waving, Ma."

She turned to wave. I put down my satchel to wave with both hands. Pa said something to the children, and they all turned and waved, too.

"*Adjo!*"

"Goodbye!"

"*Adjo!*"

"*Adjo!*"

The farewells echoed back and forth across the barnyard.

Ma was the first to turn back toward the road.

Just beyond the fields Pa and Olaf had plowed this spring were the Iversons' fields, plowed in curving lines that outlined each gentle rise in the land. As we approached their house and barn, I tightened my grip on my satchel and lifted my chin. While Erick Iverson was measuring his wheat, I was off to see the country, nearly coast to coast. I would not look back.

CHAPTER 5

ON THE ROAD

May 6, 1896–Day 1

Mica Creek to Spring Valley

PUFFS of breeze cooled my cheeks as we set off along familiar roads. The air smelled like plowed wheat fields and budding lilacs. A meadowlark sang. This was the beginning of the biggest adventure of my life. At least that's what I told myself. I veered between giddy excitement and terror.

We were just walking twenty-five miles today. Except for the weight of the seven-pound satchel in my hand, the tug of the canteen strap on my shoulder, and the knowledge that I was carrying a pistol instead of textbooks in my bag, today would be just like a walk to school in Spokane. For seven months I would not be herding younger brothers and sisters through their chores and schoolwork. I would not be scrubbing floors or boiling overalls or canning tomatoes. Without slowing my pace, I leaned over to break off sprigs of Queen Anne's lace and chicory by the side of the road.

Ma watched as I tucked the flowers behind one ear. "You'll look like a gypsy," she said.

I snapped off another sprig of Queen Anne's lace and tucked it behind my other ear. If I was going to discover the gypsy in my soul, I was not going to do it in half measures.

Just then I caught sight of Mrs. Youngquist, who had popped out of her kitchen door and was headed toward the hen house.

Ma waved, but Mrs. Youngquist did not wave back.

"She can hardly wait to see us give up and come home next week so she can say 'I told you so,'" I said.

"*Ja*, well," Ma said. "Mrs. Youngquist will have to wait until Mica Creek runs backward. We'll reach New York and come back famous, with more money than she'll see in her lifetime."

Ma squinted at the road ahead, but there was nothing to see but Mrs. Youngquist's chore yard, more wheat fields, and an empty road. "Once word gets out on this walk, our path will be lined with people cheering us on."

I snorted. "And I suppose you think we'll have a brass band at each railroad station and the mayor's wife will be standing on the platform with an armful of roses for you." I was surprised Ma didn't have us carrying placards reading HELGA ESTBY, TRANSCONTINENTAL PEDESTRIAN and a trumpet to announce our arrival at each whistle stop.

"Don't you laugh now," Ma said. "When we land on Manhattan, we'll have to dodge all the newspaper and magazine photographers wanting a picture of us."

We passed Soderstrand's farm, Lingren's farm, Fosberg's farm, and the nearly finished house that my friend Tilda would be moving into when she married Carl next month.

When we finally reached the railroad tracks, I tried to keep my new boots out of the dirt and my skirts out of the sagebrush by walking from railway tie to railway tie, only to discover that the train's water closets dumped directly onto the tracks. After the first hundred yards of muttering *Uff da!* (as in "I almost stepped in it") and *ISH DA!* (as in "I *did* step in it"), I gave up, leaving the tracks to pick my path alongside Ma, several feet away from the line.

Ma stopped for a moment to tighten her shoelaces. When she straightened, she reached out to smooth my bangs. "If you aren't used to using the curling iron, you should have let me do it for you."

I pulled her hand away from my hair. "They'll loosen up by themselves." I already knew I'd turned them into sheep's wool instead of a reasonable copy of Nellie Bly's bangs. I didn't need Ma to tell me so.

As we continued, Ma chattered on about her high-flying fantasies of how we'd spend the fortune we hadn't yet won. I suspected it was her way of keeping her mind off the memory of Lilly reaching her arms out to her as we had turned to leave home. I traded hands again on my satchel, trying to delay blisters on my palms, but I couldn't trade off feet. I could already feel blisters rising there, erupting like bubbles on over-risen bread. I was relieved when we reached the Union Pacific station house at Hope. Without any deference to Ma, I plopped down in the only chair.

Ma dropped her satchel with a thump and stood over me while I started to unlace my shoes. "If your feet are swelling, you better not take off your boots. You'll never get them back on again."

"My feet aren't swelling," I said. "My new boots are just stiff." I found my spare socks and put them on over the pair I was already wearing, carefully avoiding contact with my blisters.

"*Ja*, well," she said. "I told you to break them in better." Ma had been smart to wear her comfortable old chore boots, which would be sturdy enough to carry her the first few hundred miles.

"*Ja*, well," I said as I forced my boots back on. "I wanted them to last longer on the road." I wiped dust off the toes and tightened the shoelaces so the heels wouldn't rub so much.

Just then I felt a gentle splat on my scalp. I looked up, thinking I had been the target of a passing hawk. Three more drops fell on my upturned face.

Ma held out one hand. "Just a spring spit of rain," she said.

I opened my satchel and shook out my oilskin poncho. "It can rain hard this time of year."

"Nonsense," Ma said. "This sprinkle will be over before

you slip on that poncho and you'll just have to pack it away again."

We got back on the road, me with my poncho, Ma without. After ten minutes of rainy mist, the sun reappeared and a rainbow arced across the road before us. "See, what did I tell you?" Ma nearly strutted with the satisfaction of being right. "Nothing can keep us down, Clara. I tell you, that rainbow is our sign that this trip is meant to be, and we'll have good weather from here to New York."

But she didn't get to gloat for long. As the rainbow started to fade, another drop of rain hit my nose. Half a mile later, the spring spit of rain became a downpour. While I waited for Ma to scramble into her poncho, I tugged down Pa's fisherman's hat, crushing the flowers I'd put in my hair earlier. I squinted through the raindrops on my eyelashes at the gunmetal-gray sky and the miles of open land. I felt small, as vulnerable as a field mouse in a freshly plowed field with an eagle circling overhead.

Even in ponchos and oilskin hats, we got soaked. Rainwater and mud collected on the bottoms of our skirts with every step. Rain trickled down the ties of my hat and under the wide neck of my poncho.

We continued on in silence to Latah Creek, which was already becoming a river, and on to the Waverley station. This time there was a bench big enough for the two of us under the veranda roof. We had covered fourteen miles so far.

While Ma took out our sandwiches, I eased off my boots and socks. The skin was already rubbing off the tops of the nickel-size blisters on my heels, dime-size blisters on the sides of my little toes, and half-dollar-size blisters on the balls of my feet. I retrieved the bottle of iodine from my first-aid kit, wincing just to think how it was going to sting, and steeled myself to dab the glass wand across the raw, oozing mess on my feet. I padded each blister with a wad of cotton wool secured with adhesive bandage.

Ma watched in silence, holding both sandwiches in her hands. "*Ja*, well," she said. To her credit, she said no more aloud, but it was clear what she was thinking.

"*Ja*, well," I muttered. At least I'd had the sense to put on my poncho and try to keep dry when it started to rain.

We ate our boiled egg and butter sandwiches washed down with swigs of water. My canteen was half empty already. By tomorrow I'd have sipped the last of the water from our own well at home.

After finishing my sandwich, I spread out the newspaper it had been wrapped in to read the bits of articles on it.

Ma folded her scrap of newspaper and brushed her skirt of crumbs as she stood. "I'm happy to see you reading the newspaper instead of those novels. About time you took an interest in the real world."

"I get enough of the real world in my own life," I said. "I'm only reading the newspaper scrap because that's all there is to read." I eased my feet back into my boots and reluctantly stood. "Did you see an outhouse, Ma?" I started to look for a wastebasket for the newspaper, but Ma stopped me.

"You might be needing that," she said.

She approached the outhouse behind the station cautiously, knocked, then used the hem of her skirt to open the door.

We'd have to keep an eye out for old newspapers, it seemed, and not so we could keep up on current events.

By the time the sun—what I could see of it behind the clouds—was low on the horizon, the rain had slackened to a limp drizzle. As we tromped along, the vague bump on the landscape gradually took on the crisp outline of a grain elevator.

"That must be Rosalia, Ma!" Rosalia was twenty-six miles from Mica Creek, a mile over our day's quota. "This would be a good place to stop, wouldn't it?"

"We could go a few more miles, couldn't we?" Ma said. She trod on stolidly as if she could see right through the Rockies and across the plains to that ten thousand dollars waiting for her in New York. I suspected if I didn't make us stop at a reasonable hour each night, she would have us walking twenty hours a day until we both dropped dead.

Just beyond the town proper, another lantern flickered to life in a window not too far from the tracks. "That's probably the last house in town. If we don't find someone to take us in soon, we'll end up nesting in the fields like quail."

Ma glanced down at my feet. "If you're tired."

As we approached the house and picked our way through the muddy chore yard, I was encouraged by a window box of pansies. A person who tended flowers was bound to be nice, wasn't she? I slowed down as we approached the porch. Although I was looking forward to dinner and a dry place to sleep, I'd rather sleep in a haystack than beg for a bed as if we were tramps.

Ma squeezed my shoulder. "They'll take us in, you'll see. It's the law of the frontier to take in a stranger on the road." She tidied her hair and practiced a smile before raising her hand to knock on the front door.

An older woman, as small as Ida, opened the door a crack. "Are you alone?"

"Yes, it's just me and my daughter," said Ma. "Could we get out of the rain while we introduce ourselves?" She edged toward the doorway, but I hovered behind, poised to head back to the road if we weren't welcomed in. "I'm Helga Estby, and this is Clara. We're walking across the country to New York City to save our farm."

"New York! You must be daft," the woman said.

Ma didn't deny that she was daft, but went on with her pitch. "Your house looked like such a friendly little place, I just knew someone nice lived here, someone who wouldn't turn a mother and her daughter out into the rain."

My stomach rumbled as the smell of food wafted through

the open door. Looking over Ma's shoulder, I saw a steaming kettle hanging over the fireplace. How I longed for the warmth of that fire.

"If we could just come inside," Ma said, "I'll show you an article about us from the *New York World* and our letter of recommendation from the mayor of Spokane."

The woman sighed and backed away from the doorway. "Even fools deserve a place out of the rain. Come on in, the two of you."

I nearly stumbled into Ma in my eagerness to get inside.

The woman held out a hand. "Mabel Philson," she said. She might not have weighed ninety-five pounds, but her grip was strong.

As I put down my bag and rolled the kinks out of my shoulders, I assessed our surroundings. The house was just one room with a loft, no bigger than our old sod house. Mrs. Philson had no store-bought furniture, no clock, and the curtains were stitched from feed sacks.

Ma took the oilskin packet out of her bag and showed Mrs. Philson the newspaper article with our picture. "See?" she said. "That's us, though I suppose we look more like drowned rats than respectable ladies after this day on the road. And here's our letter from Mayor Belt."

Mrs. Philson ran one finger over the City of Spokane seal embossed on the top of the mayor's stationery. She slowly read the letter aloud.

To Whom It May Concern:

The bearer hereof, Mrs. H. Estby, has been a resident of this city and vicinity for the last nine years, is a lady of good character and reputation, and I take pleasure in commending her and her daughter, with whom she travels, to the kindly consideration of all persons with whom they may come in contact.

> *H. N. Belt*
> *Mayor of Spokane*

Mrs. Philson returned the letter to Ma. "I guess you're official," she said. "Come have some soup."

I put a hand over my stomach to stifle another loud rumble. Fortunately, it didn't take long for her to serve up three bowls of steaming broth along with the last of her bread, which was so hard that I had to dunk it in the soup to chew it. Mrs. Philson watched us eat every bite. I'm not sure if she was anxious to see that we liked it, or wished she could have had more of it herself. It was hard to enjoy the food, knowing she had so little to share.

After dinner, Mrs. Philson loaned us a couple of her dead husband's long shirts so we could get out of our wet things and hang them over chairs by the fire to dry. I put the pan of left-over hot dishwater on the floor and soaked my feet in it while recording our first day's events in my journal.

Ma seemed reinvigorated by the food and change of company and tried to spark a political discussion with Mrs. Philson.

"Are you hoping Major McKinley or Mr. Bryan will be our next president?" she asked.

"Last I heard, neither one of them can control the weather," Mrs. Philson said, without looking up from her hands and knees as she mopped up the puddles of water growing under our petticoats and skirts. Ma picked up another rag and got down on the floor to help. I knew I should have joined them, but if I got up I'd leave a trail of blood-tinged footprints on the floor they were trying to clean.

"I can't vote, so why should I waste time thinking about who sits in the White House?" Mrs. Philson looked sideways at Ma. For a moment both their faces glowed in the firelight.

"If any man can vote, don't you deserve the vote, too?"

Ma was launching into one of her standard suffragist speeches. I suspected Mrs. Philson wasn't interested, but there was no stopping Ma once she'd started. I turned back to my journal.

Soaked skirts, sore feet, and begging for a dry spot to spend the night. Is that all I'd have to write about every day? How could I do this for another seven months?

Day One on the way to New York City
Mica Creek to Freeman — 2 miles
Freeman to Hope — 5 miles
Hope to Waverley (crossed Latah Creek) — 7 miles
Waverly to Spring Valley — 7 miles
Spring Valley to Rosalia — 5 miles
Only 3,974 miles to go.

CHAPTER 6

EARNING OUR WAY

May 7, 1896–Day 2
Rosalia to Saint John

OUR clothes had dried overnight, but with today's rain and wind they wouldn't stay that way for long. Mercifully, Ma was less talkative today. She told our story anew to everyone we passed, but in between she was generally quiet. Since my feet needed no instruction from my brain, I cast about for some project to keep my mind busy. "Ma, can I borrow Pa's watch?"

"Why would you need to know the time here?" She gestured toward the miles of plowed fields on either side of the tracks.

"I'll tell you when I have it figured out," I said.

"*Ja*, well." She set her satchel down on a rocky patch out of the mud and slipped the cord with Pa's pocket watch over her head. She handed it to me with both hands. "Don't drop it," she said.

I took it just as carefully, slipping the cord over my own head and checking the time. "It's nine thirty-four," I said. "Just walk normally. And don't talk or you'll make me lose count." We resumed our pace as I mumbled the number of my steps, periodically checking the hands of the watch.

At nine forty-four I announced, "Nine hundred and ninety-three steps."

"Well, that fact will make a fascinating entry for our journals," Ma said.

"Don't laugh, Ma. If anyone wants to know how many steps it takes to get from Mica Creek to New York City or how many steps we take in a day, we can tell them. I walk about three miles an hour. If I take nearly a thousand steps in ten minutes, I'll take nearly two thousand steps in the twenty minutes it takes to walk a mile. To cover our quota of twenty-five miles a day, we'll take fifty thousand steps. And, since we can't walk as the crow flies, we'll probably walk at least four thousand miles getting to New York. That's at least eight million steps." I stopped long enough to wipe a few drops of rain off Pa's watch and give it back to Ma.

"Nearly eight million steps." Ma's face drooped for a moment, then brightened. "That's pretty impressive, *nei*?"

My gap-toothed grin answered Ma's as I held up my canteen in a toast. "Here's to eight million!"

Ma tapped my canteen with her own. "Eight million!"

Uff da! As one foot landed awkwardly in a puddle, muddy water soaked the one dry area left on my skirts and spoiled fantasies of newspaper headlines celebrating our eight million-step walk to New York. Rain sluiced so hard down the brim of my hat, it was like looking through a waterfall. Was it just yesterday morning that I had tucked flowers in my hair and danced down the road like a gypsy?

The rest of the day was more of the same. Another fifty thousand steps. Another twenty-five miles past fields and farmhouses. When my feet hurt so bad that I was ready to plop down in a mud puddle to rest, we came to a handful of houses at Saint John. "Couldn't we stop here for the night?" I asked. Ma kept walking.

By the time we reached the next isolated house, I was limping on both feet. From the outside, it was hard to tell what kind of folks lived in this place. The barn was unpainted and the door to the outhouse was half off its hinges. A shovel had been left out in the rain and was propped up against the ramshackle hen house. But the kitchen garden looked like it had been laid out with a ruler and a pot of blooming geraniums showed through the lamp-lit window.

A woman answered the door, holding a baby. Inside,

clotheslines strung just below the ceiling were covered with drying diapers. The woman raised her eyebrows in surprise.

"You two look half drowned!" she said as she opened the door wider.

Her husband quickly joined her at the door. He scowled as he craned his neck to peer behind us into the dusk. Perhaps he thought we were in cahoots with someone bent on stealing their silverware.

We huddled together on their porch, trying to fit under the scant overhang above the door. Ma forced a laugh. "We must look a sight, but we're respectable women walking across the country to save our farm. Wouldn't you feel good knowing you'd helped us out?"

"Where's your husband?" the man asked.

"He's at home with the rest of our children," Ma explained. "My daughter and I intend to show that women are just as capable as any man by making this trip on our own."

He looked as skeptical as the reporter in Spokane about our fitness to walk clear across the country. Furthermore, he didn't look impressed that Ma was out trying to prove she was the equal of any man. Since optimism seemed to have blunted Ma's ability to read the signs, she plowed on. She held out her hand. "I'm Helga Estby, and this is Clara."

The woman shifted the baby in her arms and edged far enough forward to shake Ma's hand. The man still squinted at us like he was trying to figure out what to make of us.

Ma glanced from one face to the other and forced even more hearty goodwill into her voice. "We're going to write a book about our adventures, and if we had your names we could put you in it." She shook my elbow. "Clara, get out your notebook so you can write down the names of these nice folks."

From their expressions, I could almost see him shaking his head no and his wife timidly nodding yes. I looked up the section road toward the tracks. There wasn't another lamp-lit window or trail of chimney smoke in sight. Desperation put my tongue in gear.

"We don't mean to be a burden on you," I said. "We can work for our keep. Just name what you need done and we'll do it."

At hearing my voice, Ma looked at me as if she had found a mouse spouting Latin. My heart stopped beating while I waited to see if my offer would be accepted.

The man finally smiled, but it wasn't the kind of smile that made me want to smile back. "I'm Mr. Ramsey," he said. "And Mrs. Ramsey, and little Rebecca. Maybe we can think of something. Something especially fitting for two women out to prove they're equal to any man."

Thankfully it was the wrong time of year for butchering hogs, but what else did he have in mind?

He led us off the porch and back into the mud to a heap of logs that had been roughly chopped into wood-stove lengths. "Know how to swing an ax?" he asked. Without waiting for an answer, he trotted straight back toward his warm kitchen.

"Do you have any gloves?" I called. He was halfway back to the house already, so he must not have heard me.

Ma drew in her shoulders against the wind and rain as she eyed the jumbled woodpile. "If you'd just given me another minute I could have talked him around without having to chop wood."

"I don't think so, Ma," I said.

"I wonder how much he means for us to chop?"

"Maybe we could satisfy him just by showing we can swing an ax without losing a foot," I said. I tilted my head toward the window facing the chore yard. Mr. Ramsey's weasel-like face poked between the curtains, watching us. I felt like sticking my tongue out at him. "If he thinks he's going to get a laugh watching us bumble around figuring out which end of an ax goes where," I said, "I'll show him what the New Woman is made of."

While I swung the ax, Ma stacked. I whacked and chopped like the fate of the world hung on my getting through the whole pile by nightfall. By the end of a quarter hour, I was as damp from my own sweat as from the rain, and I handed over the ax to Ma. For Mr. Ramsey's benefit I tried not to look like my arms were as wobbly as jelly. The stack of chopped wood grew more slowly during my second shift with the ax, and slower still on my third. Sometime along the way, Mr. Ramsey's face disappeared from the window.

By the end of an hour, there was just enough daylight left to compare the blisters on our hands. Ma plopped down on the low end of our solidly stacked pile. "Don't you think we've done enough?"

Just then, Mrs. Ramsey dashed out in the rain. "Come get warm before you catch your death," she said. "Mr. Ramsey has already had his supper and has gone to bed. He himself would never chop more than a day's worth of wood in this rain."

Once inside, she clucked over our hands. "I have just the thing." She took down a large can from an open shelf in the kitchen. "Mutton tallow with chickweed, calendula flowers, and beeswax."

We held out our hands as she gingerly dabbed the concoction on our blisters. I begged for more of her home remedy for my feet.

After Mrs. Ramsey's doctoring and two bowls of rabbit stew each, I felt like I might live to see another morning.

"Wash-up can wait," Mrs. Ramsey said. "Let's just visit." We sat on the floor next to her and admired her sleeping baby.

"I've had ten," Ma said. "Eight still living." She brought one finger within a hair's breadth of the baby's cheek and then pulled it back. "Don't want to wake her," she whispered with a smile.

"Eight children," Mrs. Ramsey said. "And how long will you be gone?" I couldn't tell if she sympathized with Ma for having to leave her children or was aghast that she'd left behind so many.

"Seven months," Ma said. "But they're all good children; they'll be fine." Her forehead knitted in a flash of worry. Then she nodded as if to convince herself, as well as Mrs. Ramsey, that they would be fine. "My oldest boy is already working in Spokane and my second-oldest daughter, Ida, is at home to help with the younger ones." Ma was silent for a moment, then stood. "Would you like to see how we mean to go?"

Mrs. Ramsey's eyes lit up at that. "I sure would!" she said.

Ma got out her maps and showed her our route and the sights we hoped to see. They traded the trials of teething babies and rain that came at the wrong time just before harvest. Ma told her the remedy she'd used for Henry's colic when he was a baby, and Mrs. Ramsey gave Ma the name of someone she knew who'd moved fifteen miles south of Rosalia who could give us lunch tomorrow.

They were still chatting away when I got ready for bed and lay down on the blankets Mrs. Ramsey had laid out for us. Just as I was about to drift off, I caught one last comment from Mrs. Ramsey.

"I've never been more than eleven miles from this place, myself," she said.

CHAPTER 7

A FIFTY-MILE DAY

May 8, 1896–Day 3
Saint John to La Crosse

FOR the third day in a row, it rained. The only things not dampened were Ma's spirits. She babbled on about how surprised Mr. Ramsey would be by the neat stack of wood we'd left for him and how he'd think differently about the New Woman from now on. My own spirits, however, were soggy. I was too tired from chopping wood and walking twenty-odd miles yesterday to face Ma's chatter, so I walked by myself on the other side of the tracks, far enough away to discourage conversation. At least today's mud gradually softened my boots, which had dried overnight as hard as copper-plated baby shoes.

* * *

We had lunch with Mrs. Ramsey's friend, and walked another ten miles before looking for a family to take us in. We were greeted at the first place by a stubble-faced man holding a rifle like a walking stick. After a glance at the rifle, Ma bravely launched into her speech. "We're walking to New York to save our family's farm," she began. Her voice was strong, but I detected a slight quaver as her eyes darted down again to the rifle.

"No decent woman would be tromping across the country without her husband. Go home where you belong!" he said. The door slammed in our faces.

"*Uff da,*" I muttered. I grabbed a handful of waterlogged skirt, picked up my satchel, and stepped down from the porch. Mud oozed over the tops of my boots and seeped down to my toes. Like anybody who worked on a farm, I'd been wet and dirty before, but I'd always had food and a bed to look forward to at the end of the day. Under Ma's "the Lord will provide" approach, we carried no food, and in this part of the state it might be ten miles to shelter.

As we continued walking, my stomach growled. "Do you think we'll get food at the next station?"

Ma sighed. "We'll just have to keep walking and find out," she said.

Maybe the next station was just around the next curve in the tracks. I rubbed the head of the owl in my pocket for good luck.

Two hours later, maybe three, the clouds parted enough to reveal a half moon. I goaded myself on, chanting just one more step, one more. What foolish pride had made me think I was destined for a better life than Mica Creek? I'd starve as a writer, and the chances of my becoming a governess for Mr. Rochester, like Jane Eyre, or winning the heart of a Mr. Darcy, like Elizabeth Bennet, were exceedingly slim. Erick wasn't my soul mate, but he was cheerful and hard-working. He would never treat a stranger like Mr. Ramsey or the man with the rifle had treated us.

I perked up when the faint light picked out the outline of a water tower less than a mile ahead, but when we reached the water tower we wilted. There was no station house. Yet another two hours on, we passed another water tower without a station house.

About two miles past Winona, we stumbled up the steps to the veranda of the La Crosse railroad station. Under cover at last, we wrung our skirts, scraped our boots, and shook out our ponchos.

Ma opened the door. "Anybody here?"

I crept into the waiting room behind her, expecting someone with a railroad badge to pop out from behind a bench and tell us we were trespassing on Union Pacific property. I held my breath, listening.

Bedsprings squeaked in the room behind the door on one end of the waiting room. The door opened and a sleep-wrinkled man in trousers and unbuttoned railroad uniform shirt peered out. "Where on earth did you come from? It's miles to the closest house. And..." he said as he pulled out his railroad watch, "it's one-oh-seven in the morning! The next train in either direction isn't due through here for five hours."

"We're not taking the train," Ma said. "We're walking."

"This waiting room is for the use of Union Pacific passengers." He looked down to see that we were standing in puddles of our own making. I was shivering hard enough to break a molar.

"We've walked fifty miles today," Ma said.

I did some quick figuring. If this was La Crosse, we'd only walked forty-three miles. But if she was stretching the truth to save our lives, I wouldn't quibble.

The stationmaster scratched his head. "It's against the rules," he said. "But I can't turn you out on a night like this. You can have the waiting room to yourselves until six a.m., but then I'll have to come back out to get ready for the first train."

We spread our petticoats and ponchos over the backs of the waiting room benches to dry, then loosened our corsets. A hard wooden bench had never felt so good.

May 10, 1896 – Day 5

La Crosse to Hay

⌒⌒⌒

While Ma and I took turns dodging raindrops to the outhouse, the stationmaster, Mr. Willis, stoked the trash-burner stove and prepared breakfast.

When Mr. Willis started to get out three cups, Ma held out a forestalling hand. "Clara's too young for coffee," she said. She didn't know I'd treated myself to a cup almost every morning when she was in bed this winter. The aroma of real coffee — not chicory — and the thought of cold fingers around a warm cup were more than I could bear. "Mr. Willis, I'd like some, too."

"Stimulants aren't good for you," Ma said. She sighed a put-upon sigh and looked to Mr. Willis for sympathy for having to deal with such a wayward, contrary daughter.

I sighed a put-upon sigh, too. How could I keep up with Ma today without some stimulation?

Mr. Willis glanced back and forth between Ma's disapproving look and my longing one. He decided in my favor. "Sure enough," he said. "A cold, wet day needs coffee."

All through breakfast, Mr. Willis had that poised-to-say-something look a shy person has when he's itching to ask you something but is waiting for the right way to put it. I knew that feeling, because it was one I often had myself. As we put down our forks, he finally came out with it.

"Are either of you good with a darning needle?" he asked. "Every sock I own has heels worn thin and a hole in the toe, and I got wash piled up, too. I never quite got the hang of laundry."

I looked at Ma to see what she thought. I wasn't going to have her blaming me for roping us into more work again. I took her wry smile to mean that as tired as we were, we owed him something for breakfast.

While Ma caught up in her journal and curled her hair, I washed and hung clothes by the Franklin stove to dry over backs of chairs. Although the socks were still damp, Ma darned them while I explored the station.

Mr. Willis had a mahogany roll-top desk stacked with canvas-bound ledgers against one wall, and a flat-topped desk for his telegraph key. When a train stopped, he exchanged pouches of ingoing and outgoing mail and helped unload a coffin and boxes from Montgomery Ward. He was matter-of-fact about the coffin, as if handling dead bodies was no different than piling boxes of blue willow dinner plates or cultivators. I stared at the coffin, wondering who was in it. If Ma and I died on this trip, would Miss Waterson pay to have us shipped back home to Mica Creek, or would we have to be buried where we dropped?

I sat on a bench outside the station and watched the sun climb halfway to noon. Using a yard or so of rope I'd begged from Mr. Willis, I tied a long handle onto my satchel so it could ride on either shoulder. Even if I still had foot blisters, maybe my hands would heal. I offered to make a strap for Ma, but she said the shoulder strap would wrinkle the shoulder on her jacket, and that carrying the satchel by hand was more genteel.

Since we weren't starting until noon, we only planned to walk fifteen miles to the next station today. I didn't know if Mr. Willis was grateful for clean, darned clothes or he just felt sorry for us, but he telegraphed the stationmaster in Hay to ask him to find us a real bed to sleep in tonight. If word got out we were willing to do laundry in exchange for bed and bread, we might be doing a lot of laundry.

May 16 and 17, 1896 – Days 11 and 12

Walla Walla, Washington

As we approached Walla Walla, the sun's rays found gaps between the clouds to shine on miles of rolling hills, covered thickly with well-sprouted wheat instead of sage and rock. Pa would have given his eyeteeth for crops that came in that lush.

Between the joy of walking in dry clothes and anticipating the first town big enough for its own newspaper, Ma was building herself up to a tizzy. "Do you think they'll want to take our picture? Will the mayor of Walla Walla want to meet us?"

I just wondered if we'd find food and a bed tonight.

At the newspaper office, Ma handed the reporter one of her *cartes de visite*.

"Mrs. H. Estby and daughter, Pedestrians. Spokane to New York," he read. His eyes flicked back and forth between the postcard-size picture of us in the black silk dresses we'd donned at the photographer's studio and the muddy vision we presented to him now.

"You must be 'and daughter,'" he said, nodding in my direction as I pretended to peruse a back issue of the *Union* from the stack on the counter. I supposed he was inviting me to say something, but if I opened my mouth, I'd probably put my elbow in it. Besides, Ma had seen fit to put only her name on the cards; she could provide the fodder for his article.

He shrugged and turned back to Ma. "You're really walking all the way to New York?" He cocked his head, probably trying to decide whether Ma was crazy or heroic.

Ma gave the same speech she'd given in Spokane, and seemed gratified that the reporter was impressed that we would win ten thousand dollars if we reached New York by November 30. She watched as he wrote down the part about the money. "Mention also that we have to earn our own way as we go, so we are open for any odd job," she said.

Ma caught my eyes peeping above the newspaper and gave me a conspiratorial smile. "Except chopping wood," she added.

I lowered the newspaper far enough for her to see my answering grin.

CHAPTER 8

INDIAN ENCOUNTERS

May 18, 1896–Day 13

Union Pacific Railway Station, Pendleton, Oregon

WE STOPPED for the day at the Pendleton station, near the edge of the Umatilla Reservation. While I waited for Ma to finish washing up, I poked through the wire rack of postcards picturing local Indians. The train tracks we followed would lead us right into the reservation tomorrow, which meant that for a day — the whole day and maybe into the night — we would be on foot, without cavalry escort, surrounded by Indians. Was I scared? A little. But maybe I had just read too many Deadwood Dick stories. Anyway, by now I was looking forward to an adventure, as long as it was one I would live to tell.

"Everybody goes for that card, the Cayuse papooses."

As I whirled to see who had crept up on me, the card slid from my fingers. I was too embarrassed to look at the man's face, but glimpsed his crisply pressed blue railway uniform as I bent to retrieve the card. His black shoes had been polished to such a shine I could almost see my face redden in them. Just as I reached toward the card, he swooped down and plucked it from the floor, nearly bumping heads with me. We both quickly straightened.

He held out the card and pointed to the picture of howling twins laced onto their cradleboards. "Tox-e-lox and A-lompum," he said. He pronounced the names with deep-throat clicks that would need a whole new alphabet to get recorded in my journal. "Cayuse names."

"Ma and I have to walk across the reservation tomorrow," I said.

I looked at him for reassurance that we would be safe. His bristly black hair broke out on both sides of his railway cap in cowlicks in spite of an effort to pomade it smooth. His eyes were a gentle brown, the color of walnuts. His cheekbones were high and sharp, like Laplanders from the north of Norway…

Or Indians! I stumbled back a step.

Confirming that my suspicion was correct, he spun the rack and pulled off another postcard. "This is my grandmother," he said.

I bent forward to look at the card, then jerked upright when I realized how close it brought my face to his hand. His grandmother had posed in a cape, large round earrings, and headband, each intricately beaded. Her eyes were nearly lost in a web of wrinkles as she smiled.

"But you don't live on the reservation?"

"I've done lots of things you might not expect," he said. "I played trumpet in Father Grassi's brass band at Saint Anne's Mission School, and now," he said, pointing to his cap, "I work for the Union Pacific Railway. My name is Um-ka He-yute-wa-ta-low-it."

I sprained my tongue trying to say the first part of his name, then covered my mouth and shook my head with a nervous giggle.

"At least you tried to say it." He grinned. "The fathers at Saint Anne's gave up. They chose the name Luke Fletcher for me. Fletcher means 'one who makes arrows.' Father John had a sense of humor, I think."

I avoided his gaze as I slowly turned the rack, looking at pictures of an Indian school, a pile of baskets on a porch, and a young woman in fringed buckskin, her hair loosed from its braids and tumbling to her waist.

"You need to get something for your hands," he said.

I returned the postcard I'd been looking at to the rack and clasped my hands — still raw from chopping half of Mr. Ramsey's woodpile — behind my back to hide them.

"My grandmother used to make a poultice of *Chaenactis douglasii* or fleabane and wolf lichen for my rope burns."

I crossed the room, succumbing to a sudden urge to study

a map of the reservation on the side wall of the station. What was I to make of an Indian who knew the Latin names for plants, worked for the railroad, and played the trumpet in a brass band? Johnny and Arthur would never believe it!

I hadn't heard his footsteps following me to the map, but from behind my back came the soft voice again. "Don't worry about walking across the reservation tomorrow. You'll be as safe on the reservation as you would be in town, but if you don't want to take the word of an Indian on it, you should talk to Major Moorhouse, the Indian agent."

I was saved from having to make more conversation when Ma bustled through the door of the ladies' waiting room. She saw immediately what I had not and put one arm protectively around my shoulder, tugging me away from Mr. Fletcher. "Are you all right?"

Ma claimed never to have read a dime novel in her life, but I suspected her ideas of Indians — like mine — had been shaped more by the adventures of Buffalo Bill and Deadwood Dick than firsthand experience.

"I'm fine, Ma. Mr. Fletcher was just telling me about the Indian agent for the reservation, Major Moorhouse."

As we walked toward the agent's house, I couldn't believe I had met a real live Indian. Arthur, Johnny, and Billy would be jealous. Ida and Bertha would faint.

Dear Olaf, Arthur, Johnny, and Billy,
I met my first Indians today and got a close-up look at a real

teepee! An Indian woman we met had her baby in a cradleboard like the twins on this postcard. I bet Ma sometimes wished she had you laced up and out of trouble when you were little. We stayed overnight with Major Moorhouse (the Indian agent who took the pictures on these postcards) and by getting an early start, crossed the entire Umatilla Reservation in one day.

Love, Clara

P.S. Indian children have to go to school, too — and wear uniforms!

Dear Ida and Bertha,

The woman on this postcard is the grandmother of the Real Live Indian I talked to at the railway station just outside the Umatilla Reservation! Take a close look at the beadwork on the earrings, headband, and necklace, and try to imagine them in red and yellow and blue and green.

I was amazed that white settlers have farms on the reservation. You could look one direction, see a white clapboard house surrounded by plowed fields and think you were right home in Mica Creek. You'd look across the road and see a dozen teepees! I miss you both!

Love, Clara

P.S. Send me a letter with all the details from Tilda and Carl's wedding next week! Hug Billy and Lillian for me.

CHAPTER 9

IN THE BLUES

May 20, 1896–Day 15

Gibbon Station to Meacham, Oregon

As we left the Gibbon station on the far side of the reservation, Ma predicted a beautiful day for us in the Blue Mountains. For the first hour, her prediction was right. After two weeks of rain, I'd almost forgotten how blue a sky could be.

As we climbed higher, however, the air grew chilly and the wind picked up, swirling my skirt and pulling my hair out of its pins. Ma held one hand to the top of her head like she thought the wind would take off with her hair entirely. After five miles of buffeting, we were relieved to find shelter at the Duncan station.

The stationmaster assured us the brown bears in the mountains seldom attacked. All we had to do was make lots of noise as we went along and they'd most likely choose to get out of our way. "Most likely" was slim comfort. As we walked, Ma carried her squeeze bulb filled with pepper and I kept one hand on my pistol. It wouldn't kill a bear unless I got it in the eyeball, but maybe it would make enough noise to scare him off.

It was too much work to think of a steady string of things to say, even for Ma, so I started singing, and Ma joined in. The bears wouldn't care that neither of us could carry a tune. I went through all the verses of "She'll Be Coming 'Round the Mountain," followed by some rousing hymns. While I thought of what to sing next, the only sound was our shoes on gravel.

Even a rousing hymn and a brisk pace weren't enough to keep us warm as we climbed higher. We pulled on our ponchos to cut the cold, damp wind that whistled through the pass, through the trees, and through my wool skirt and cotton petticoat on its way to my bones.

When we stopped to rest, I took a sip from my canteen. "*Uff da!*" The words were muffled because my lips had half-frozen to the metal spout. I kept blowing warm air into the canteen until the spout warmed up enough to peel my mouth off the metal without losing a layer of skin. I touched my lips cautiously to reassure myself they were still there. My knees knocked in the cold. "I wish I'd brought my quilted wool petticoat and union suit," I said.

Ma dropped her satchel and pulled her hands up under her poncho. "As long as you're wishing, how about a fur muff and a sleigh with six white horses?"

"I can't come up with six white horses," I said, "but we have something to take the place of a muff." I pulled my spare socks onto my hands like mittens and held them up for Ma's approval.

"It'll do," Ma said, and put socks on her hands, too, before continuing on.

Just as I was about to remind Ma about her prediction of a lovely May walk in the mountains, I gasped.

"Look—it's like Christmas!" Light snow began to sift down from a white sky and dust the fir trees. The first flakes were damp and clumped together like teaspoon-size snowballs. I caught a clump in my mouth. In six hours we'd climbed from summer into winter.

"It won't last," Ma said. "Most of it will melt as soon as it touches the ground."

But the snow didn't melt, and the wind didn't die down. Snow accumulated inch by inch until it completely covered the tracks, covered my boots, and came up halfway to my knees. "How will we know which way to go if we can't see the tracks?" I said.

Ma clutched her satchel with both arms to keep it from being snatched away by the howling wind. Another layer of snow settled on her shoulders and the brim of her rain hat. I waited for her face to light up with an answer. Instead, her face took on that paralyzed look a deer gets when caught in a lantern's light at night. "I don't know," she said.

I brushed the snow off my eyelashes and squinted ahead.

I could just make out the next telegraph pole, and a miragelike glimpse of what was either a sparsely limbed fir tree or another pole. "The telegraph poles run alongside the tracks," I said, answering my own question. "We'll find our way."

Leaning into the wind and navigating from one telegraph pole to the next, we pushed our way through ten inches, twelve inches, fourteen inches of snow.

Finally, a sign materialized out of the haze of snow: MEACHAM STATION, ELEV. 4,055 FT. Most people would read that sign from inside the train, sipping tea or hot chocolate from porcelain cups. Not Ma and me.

I clomped up the steps to the door of the station. With icy socks on my hands, I couldn't get the door handle to turn and nearly fell into the room when a burly man in Union Pacific uniform opened the door. "Oh, golly," he said. "You look like ghosts. Not to criticize, but most people have the sense to take the train instead of walking across the Blue Mountains in a blizzard."

As I pulled Ma toward the potbelly stove, she looked like she was in shock that the weather had not behaved itself for us today. What would have happened to Ma if she had been on her own? We had armed ourselves with ponchos, a pistol, and pepper gun, but never thought we'd have to battle a snowstorm in May. What else had we neglected to prepare for?

CHAPTER 10

~~~

ALMOST JAILBIRDS

May 21, 1896–Day 16

La Grande, Oregon

Dear Arthur and Johnny,

In case you have not had your quota of dime novels this month, I am sending you a true account of our First Adventure:

Our two brave heroines are Helga Estby, a Norwegian immigrant homesteader, and her daughter Clara. For two weeks they had walked through heavy mud, swollen rivers, and rugged mountains, determined to reach New York City to win a wager that would save their family's farm.

Only the day before, the valiant women walkers had crossed the Blue Mountains in a ferocious blizzard. When the next morning dawned clear, they had no presentiment that this day would be other than an uneventful walk into La Grande, Oregon, where they hoped for the reward of a long, hot bath.

Late in the day, they came out of the foothills on the far side of the Blue Mountains. Looking down on the wheat growing in the Grande Ronde Valley, they could see the ruts left by the thousands of wagons carrying courageous pioneers westward on the Oregon Trail.

Still concentrating on their footing in the loose rock slicked by melting snow, they did not notice the slow hoofbeats behind them until they heard a man's voice. "You headed into La Grande?"

Helga Estby quickened her pace. She did not answer.

In a quick glance back, Clara observed the man's straight dark mustache, oiled hair, bowler hat, suit, and once white shirt.

"How far you two been walking?" he asked.

Clara, innocent as she was of the darker side of human nature, started to reply, but her mother warned her to keep her silence.

The man was willing to do all the talking himself, however. He slid off his horse and walked along behind the two women.

Though travel-ravaged and less clean than was their wont, their proud carriage still identified them as paragons of decent womanhood. In the gentle wind blowing southward through the valley, a strand of Clara's fair hair pulled loose from her decorous bun and glowed like a golden filament halo in the solitary ray of sun, which pierced the billowy cloud.

"Why you out here by yourselves?" His voice was coarse and menacing. He paused, inviting a reply, but the women remained silent. "You got a boyfriend, titmouse?" He drew abreast of Clara and poked his elbow into her arm to make sure she knew he was addressing her, but Clara still did not answer.

He dropped behind again and continued his one-sided conversation.

"Sure would like to see what's in them satchels. Run off with your old man's loot?"

When he shoved her mother, Clara's eyes widened in hor-

ror. Would she have to use the gun her father had insisted they carry? Her face grew hot as she fumbled in her bag to bring her gun to the top where she could grab it if she had to.

The dark-mustached man shoved Clara's back this time. As she lurched forward he jabbed her again, harder, and she fell to her hands and knees across her satchel. He grabbed her chin from behind, like a cougar snapping a sheep's head around to break its neck. As Clara flailed helplessly, he leaned over her to growl, "When I talk, look at me like you're listening."

Clara's frantic mother grabbed one of his shoulders and tried to wrench him off her daughter, but he swung one scarred fist, which landed with a thud on her brow. In spite of the trickle of blood now running into her eye, she held steadfast to the villain's arm, straining with every ounce of a mother's courage to drag him off her daughter.

He tried to shake her loose, but she would not release her grip, so he stooped to his boot, where Clara was alarmed to see the hilt of a knife. As he pulled out his glittering dagger, she pulled her gun from her satchel and before she could lose her nerve, she shot.

A hole bloomed red in his lower leg, just above the line of his boot. He howled and fell back on his posterior.

"Get on your horse and get out of here," she commanded.

She kept her gun trained on him while he limped to his horse, swearing oaths too coarse to commit to print. As he put one leg in the stirrup and swung his other, bleeding leg over the saddle, he issued a warning: "The sheriff in La Grande will throw you both in jail!"

"I doubt it," said the valiant Clara. Soon he was nothing but a dust cloud.

Clara tucked the ripped top of her skirt into her waistband and washed the cut above her mother's eye. As they walked the last two miles into town, Clara's mother took over the gun. "If there's any problem over this shooting, I'll tell the sheriff I did it," she said. "I'll not have you hung for protecting me."

Clara anxiously scanned the horizon for any sign of a posse out looking for a would-be murderess and her mother. With faith in the power of truth and the fairness of justice in this land, however, she and her mother strode directly to the sheriff's office.

As they entered the office, the man who had accosted them jabbed an accusing finger at them from his position on a rough-hewn bench. "That's them!" he shouted. "Put them in jail!"

Clara's mother slammed her satchel on the sheriff's desk and jabbed her own finger at her assailant. "That's the man who should be in jail — assaulting defenseless women . . ."

"Defenseless!" The man started to stand and groaned as his leg oozed fresh blood through the rags he had bound around it. He collapsed back on the bench and pointed to his wound. "There's all the proof you need on who should be locked up."

"How dare you . . ." Clara's mother started.

The sheriff held out one open palm against Clara's mother and the other against the man on the bench as if to physically stop the accusations and counter-accusations. "Both of you, quiet! The judge'll be through here next week, and we'll hear both of your stories then."

"But we can't stay here a week," Clara said. "We'll miss our deadline!"

"And look at us, Sheriff," Clara's mother said, pointing to her bleeding forehead and Clara's ripped skirt and bloodied hands. "We were only virtuous women defending our honor." She sorted through her bag to find her letter of recommendation from Mayor Belt of Spokane and the clipping from the New York World.

"Well," the sheriff sighed as he finished reading the article and handed it back. "I think you women are crazy for trying to walk across the country by yourselves, but it looks like you were provoked into using your gun, so I won't lock you up. In fact," he said, turning to the villain on the bench, "I am going to keep you here for a day or two. You need to keep off that leg anyway, and I'm sure these ladies would continue on easier in their minds if they knew I was keeping an eye on you."

The sheriff escorted Mrs. Estby and Clara to the door and pointed the way to his house. "My wife will see you cleaned up and mended before you're on the way. Try not to use that gun again between here and New York."

And so ends the first installment of the adventures of Helga and Clara Estby. Do you think I should change our names for the book? Helga and Clara sound more plodding than dashing.

Love,
Your gunslinging sister,
Clara

As I put down my pencil, the grim smile on my face collapsed. My arm still jangled from the recoil on the pistol, and I shuddered and gagged at the smells of gunpowder and blood, which still clung to the inside of my nose. I darted out from our host cabin long enough to retch and wash my mouth out at the pump. I could have killed that man. Or he might have killed Ma and me just to see what was in our satchels.

After a few minutes of breathing fresh air, I was ready to revise the draft of my letter to Arthur and Johnny. By this second retelling—three, if you counted the time I explained what happened to the sheriff—my heart still quickened, my ears still rang with the sound of gunshot, the bile still rose. I had an adventure to write about, but I hoped this would be the last one that nearly landed us in jail.

CHAPTER 11

THE GOVERNOR

June 5, 1896—Day 31
Boise, Idaho

E arrived at the *Idaho Daily Statesman* office still dripping trails of water from the stream we forded a few miles back where the bridge had washed out. Ma briskly shook off her poncho and fished in her satchel for one of her cards. As soon as the reporter found his notebook, she launched into her "why we're walking" spiel.

Since she was determined to be an example of indomitable womanhood, she did not complain about our walking conditions this month. I didn't complain out loud, but shivered theatrically and wrung my skirt out on the floor. Littered as the floor was with dead cigars and slimy tobacco cuds that had missed the spittoons, my wrung-out rainwater undoubtedly improved the hygiene of the office. When Ma scowled my direction, I lifted one foot to show her the sole of my shoe, which was almost thin enough to see my sock through. After crossing the Blue and Boise Mountains and walking wet for twenty-eight days, my boots were ready to be given to a teething puppy to finish off. Ma rolled her eyes and sighed, but ended her talk by saying that we planned to stay long enough to earn money for new shoes and would be grateful for a place to stay.

The next morning we found Governor McConnell's office, but he was out visiting the site of a new irrigation program. It escaped me how there could be a square inch of Idaho that needed more water.

The governor's secretary tried to shoo us out, but Ma would not be shooed. She unfolded her letter of recommendation from Spokane's Mayor Belt and held it close to his spectacles.

Ma had his attention, but I'm not sure it was favorable. I drew back, trying to make myself invisible.

Ma said she needed to see the governor. Just for a minute. Just to get his signature on the bottom of her letter from Mayor Belt.

Mr. Frisk sighed and said that if we could come back the day after tomorrow at 4:45 p.m., we could see him for five minutes and get his signature.

As we walked up Main Street and passed the Assay Office, Ma daydreamed aloud about all the gold and silver that had passed through that office over the last thirty years. I remembered two years ago, when Ma read Pa every article in the newspaper about gold strikes in Colorado and hectored him about finding us a mine. We were in mining country now, but I was more intrigued by water from the hot springs that was pumped into town to heat the houses. No chopping wood for heat!

At the post office, Ma mailed her first journal home so she wouldn't have to carry it and we picked up mail. No exciting news. Ida was taking my place as maid of honor in my friend Tilda's wedding and Bertha would be playing the piano. Arthur was still helping out while Pa's back continued to mend. He asked me to say hello to any Indian chiefs I met and to make sure Butch Cassidy didn't rob us. Erick also wrote.

Dear Clara,

More than one night I've thought of you and your mother so far from home without a man at your side to keep you safe. If your mother's agreement didn't go against it, you know I would gladly have walked from Mica Creek to New York with you. Folks in Mica Creek say your mother is irresponsible to leave her children on such a foolhardy venture, but you may be sure I defend you for your decision to go with her. I admire your loyalty, although I regret that it delays the day we can be married.

Sincerely,
Erick

Blisters and mud had taken my mind off the wedding everyone seemed to expect as soon as Ma and I returned to Mica Creek. Pa favored the match. Erick could work sixteen hours straight in the field. My brothers liked Erick; he laughed at their silliest jokes and taught them rope tricks. He was already close to fulfilling all the requirements for his own 160-acre home-stead, with good bottom land near his own Pa's farm and ours. It was a sensible match: hard-working Erick and hard-working Clara. They would have healthy, hard-working children, attend services every Sunday at the Mica Creek Lutheran Church, and be buried side by side in the Mica Creek cemetery.

When I glanced up from my letter, I caught Ma looking at me. She seemed to be waiting for my comments on his letter, but what was to tell? He was waiting, I was stalling, same as usual.

I didn't know what Pa said in his letter, but as Ma reread it, she blinked her eyes and pinched her mouth like she half wanted to cry but wouldn't. She wrote her first progress report to Miss Waterson. In the one hundred and fifty pages Ma had sent home, she had undoubtedly described every sunrise and sunset and every conversation she had had along the way. In all those pages of sunsets and conversations, she had no record of how many miles we'd walked. She had to ask me. I flipped through the pages in my own journal and added the figures in my head.

To: *Miss A. J. Waterson, 95 William Street,*
   New York City, New York

From: Helga Estby

Monthly report #1: Boise, Idaho

Miles covered, May 5–June 4: 432

Rain, mud, and blizzard in the Blue Mountains have slowed us down, but we should make up lost time here in Idaho. Shot a man in the leg but were not jailed for it.

The letter seemed powerfully short, considering all we'd been through this month, but Ma said Miss Waterson wouldn't get all the details until she paid us our ten thousand dollars. The "shot a man" line was just to whet her appetite for the rest of the story.

We spent the time waiting for the governor's signature doing laundry and gardening. With what we had left of our start-up money, we had enough to buy Ma new boots and a new journal, and socks for both of us. My shoes would have to hold together a little longer.

Four hundred and thirty-two miles this first month. At two thousand steps a mile, we had taken eight hundred and sixty-four thousand steps, but by now we should have covered nearly six hundred miles and taken over a million steps. We were already a week behind schedule.

CHAPTER 12

LOST

June 10, 1896—Day 36
Idaho

INSTEAD OF sagebrush, we had sand dunes and rocks. Instead of rain, we had hot sun. Instead of following the main line out of Shoshone, we walked eighteen miles on a spur line that came to an abrupt dead end in the foothills of the Pioneer Mountains.

"Ish da!" I said, looking at the map in the Richfield station. "We have to backtrack. We'll lose at least another day."

"Nonsense," Ma said, tracing a finger along a line between where we were and where we wanted to be. "I'm not wasting a day going back the way we came. Let's just take this shortcut directly south to get to the other track that leads to Minidoka."

"The young lady's right." The voice came from the station-master, who'd been hovering behind us as we looked at the map.

I smiled a thank-you to him for his support of the safe route along the tracks, but retracted my smile when he kept on talking.

"I don't think two ladies would be up to that rough country between here and the main line." He shook his head, as if already mourning our fate if we should try that shortcut.

As soon as he said it, I knew he'd goaded Ma into a foolhardy choice.

She puffed up in indignation. "We are not namby-pamby drawing room ladies," she said. "We crossed the Blue Mountains in a blizzard, and we can certainly walk ten miles over a few rocks to get to the other track." From the glint in her eye, I guessed it was now a matter of principle to show how strong we women could be.

So we wouldn't have to argue in front of an audience, I pulled Ma outside the station. "Ma, that shortcut could be treacherous."

"Here I come up with an idea to save half a day and you're afraid to risk it. You're as cautious as your pa." She started to fill her canteen at the station's water pump.

Filled with misgivings, I followed Ma toward Minidoka, past boulders and dry sage and gradually downward through loose rock. After an hour or so, we dead-ended at a sheer drop-off. We followed the cleft eastward, and just as we thought we had reached the end, the cleft took a sharp bend to the north, opposite of the direction we wanted to go. I dropped my bag and took out the compass Erick had given me, but poked it away again in disgust.

"Compass doesn't do much good unless you have wings to fly." I ran a finger around my collar where sweat had glued it to my neck.

Ma looked furtively at me as if she expected me to add a rebuke for not following my advice. With angelic self-restraint, I said nothing.

We'd been walking another hour when Ma blurted, "Talk! Even if it's to tell me we shouldn't have taken the shortcut."

"I guess we shouldn't have taken the shortcut! Satisfied?"

"I don't know how you came to be so much like Pa," she said. "He can get by a whole day on ten words." As she wiped her forehead with the back of a sleeve, she looked at me — really looked — as if I were a stranger she'd just met and was taking the measure of.

I didn't look much like Pa except for height. I didn't look that much like Ma, either, except for the gap between my two front teeth. Arthur had also inherited the gap, which he claimed helped him win spitting contests. I found the gap to be of no value whatsoever, except to reassure myself that I was not a foundling.

Although I didn't look like Pa, everyone said Pa was the one I took after. Like him, I would listen and gauge the other person's slant on things so I wouldn't say anything to rile them up. Since I could usually see both sides of an argument, I spent most of my time listening on the fence, a regular mugwump with my "mug" on one side of the fence and my "wump" on the other.

"If you wanted talk you should have taken Ida," I said, reaching over my shoulder to peel my sweaty shirtwaist from my back.

"Ida wouldn't have lasted an hour in this heat," Ma said. "At least you're still here."

"*Ja*, well," I answered, surprised by the compliment. "I suppose my doggedness is just another way I'm like Pa."

"*Ja*, well. You might recall that your Pa didn't want us to take this trip. Yet here you are, with me." Ma unbuttoned the first three buttons on her shirtwaist and picked up her bag, ready to walk again. "You might just be more like me than you think."

Heaven forbid, I thought.

Taking advantage of the cooler air at night, we kept walking as the stars and a sliver of moon came out. We were tired, and sharp rocks made for unsteady walking. When Ma slipped on loose rock, she threw out a hand to break her fall. She held up her left arm, watching blood drip down and soak into her sleeve. "That blood will stain if we don't wash it out right away," she said.

"I'm not wasting water on your sleeve," I said as I rinsed the sharp slash on her hand with a stingy trickle of water from the canteen. I painted on iodine, wrapped my bandanna around her palm, and helped her to a sip from the canteen. I held my own thimbleful of water in my mouth so long, there was nothing left to swallow.

Even though we had not yet made it to shelter, Ma's hand was an excuse to stop for the night. The volcanic rocks around us were as sharp as broken glass, so I mounded brush into a mattress and we lay down under the stars for the first time on our trip. With no airborne dust or moisture to dilute the starlight, the sky blossomed with more stars, brighter stars, than I had ever seen before. I tried to think of them as our guardian angels so I could relax, but sleep was a long time coming.

June 11, 1896 – Day 37
Somewhere in the Snake River lava fields

We woke in absolute quiet as the sun edged red-hot above the horizon. I took my mind off my empty stomach by writing in my journal for a few minutes. After we each took another sip of water, we started again toward Minidoka. Tall rock formations, cliffs, and crevasses detoured us from our southward course so many times that I began to feel like a croquet ball, zigzagging from wicket to wicket to reach our goals: civilization and water.

By noon, when I thought we should have reached Minidoka, I was hungry, hot, and thirsty. I sat on my satchel and fanned myself with my journal. Ma leaned over and inspected her boots, lamenting each cut and slash on her brand-new purchase.

"Three dollars wasted," she said.

I picked up my canteen and shook it at Ma's ear. "You

should be worried about water, not the state of your shoes," I said. "We only have a swallow or two left."

She didn't answer. Her eyes were sunken. Her upper chest rose and fell with laboring shudders, like that of someone with pneumonia. Her mouth opened and closed as if she were a fish out of water, but no sound came out.

Ma did not protest as I started unbuttoning her shirtwaist. "Maybe it's your cussable corset," I said. As I pulled the strings out of more and more eyelets, Ma took in enough air to talk.

"A lady always wears her corset," she wheezed.

"Ladies don't take shortcuts through the lava fields," I said, as I took off my corset, too, and dropped it into my satchel. I hadn't the energy to rebutton or retuck my shirtwaist.

As we climbed up a wrinkled river of lava stone, I kept an eye on Ma and a hand on Pa's owl. Death and I were not strangers. My brother Ole had died just days old when I was yet a toddler. We'd buried Henry this January. One of my brother Arthur's classmates was caught in a thresher, and a friend of Pa's slipped into a silo and was buried in a ton of wheat. Mrs. Rassmusson—she was only nineteen—died having her first baby, and old Mr. Ulafsson's heart stopped when he was right in the middle of his pole beans three years ago.

Ma would die someday. So would I, but I didn't expect it to be so soon, from one stupid, prideful mistake. Ma was barely lifting her feet as she walked, scraping the soles of her shoes on sharp lava rock. My head ached; the landscape tilted and blurred. But I had promised Pa I would get Ma home safely, and I wasn't one to break a promise.

We stumbled along for three more hours until we took off our skirts to pad the rocks and slept.

June 12, 1896 – Day 38
Still in the lava fields

The sun was not up yet when we woke. I tried not to think about breakfast or water as I stuffed my skirt into my satchel. The skirt was too big; ragged hems drooped over the sides, but I didn't care. I just wanted to live through that day until night, when it would cool off again. Ma's face was red and raw, and fried skin on my lips peeled off in jagged layers. We walked only a mile or two before we napped again in the shade of a rock.

After a brief rest, we staggered up. Heat bore down on us as solidly as a suit of mail. I walked with my eyes almost closed, looking through my eyelashes for a path for my feet. Walk or die, walk or die, I chanted in my head. We were probably going in circles, but as least we were proving to the turkey vultures overhead that we weren't dead yet.

I slept fitfully, with my arms around Ma, my body sheltering hers. If we died, they would find our skeletons entwined, like Quasimodo and Esmeralda. When I had read *The Hunchback of Notre Dame*, I thought it was romantic. What a fool.

June 13, 1896 – Day 39
Still in the lava fields

Into my waking dreams later that night came a ghostly wailing. Ma must have heard something, too, because her head jerked upright as she looked for the source of the sound.

Whoo-whoooo. A faint glow moved against the darkening sky. I staggered to a stand and draped Ma's left arm across my shoulders and put my right arm around her waist to support her as we picked our steps among sliding jumbles of rock. At the crest of a small rise I felt like Columbus discovering land. Far below us, the light of an engine picked out the ribbons of railroad track. We had found the route back to people and water.

We were too weak to cheer.

CHAPTER 13

THE GLORIOUS FOURTH

June 18, 1896–Day 44

On the way to Ogden, Utah

THE folks back in Minidoka had kindly rounded up secondhand boots to replace the ones we had ruined in the lava fields, but the shoes they found for me were bigger than Pa's and I had to stuff the toes and wear two pairs of socks to keep them from flopping on my feet. I felt like a clumsy puppy tripping over my outsize paws.

We followed the Bear River across the border into Utah as far as Trenton, then headed south to Cache and back up more hills to Collinston. South of Brigham, we walked along the western slopes of the Wasatch Range through scattered farms and orchards. The air hummed with bees during the day. The evenings were abuzz with mosquitoes as determined to suck my body dry as Varney the Vampire in that penny dreadful *The Feast of Blood.* Not that I usually read that sort of thing. Three years ago, a classmate had left behind a copy under her desk and I slipped it between my own textbooks and stayed up all night reading before returning it the next day.

Ma said she had a surprise waiting for us in Salt Lake City and showed me the letter she had just written to the woman who owned a progressive women's clothing store there:

July 3, 1896

Dear Miss Jones,

Please reserve time to take in the seams on the bicycling outfits you ordered in for us based on our measurements of two months ago. We expect to arrive in Salt Lake City on July 8, so our talk and exhibition can be scheduled accordingly.

Sincerely,
Helga Estby

"What talk? What exhibition?" My stomach churned with questions, but Ma said only that Miss Jones was a friend of one of her suffrage society friends in Spokane.

"Just another example of what a little hoopla can accomplish," she said.

Ma also wrote out her next monthly report. I had to give her the miles again.

To: Miss A. J. Waterson, 95 William Street,
     New York City, New York

From: Helga Estby

Monthly Report #2: Ogden

Miles covered, June 5–July 3: 317

We were lost in the Snake River lava fields for three days
and were in a sorry state when we found our way out; it took
us two days to recover. We hereby request a five-day extension
of time.

July 4, 1896 – Day 60
Ogden, Utah

I hovered over Ma as she used a borrowed paintbrush and black paint to letter a sign. "We can't waste time marching in a parade today!" I said. "Nearly a third of our time is up and we've only walked seven hundred and forty-nine miles."

Ma tidied up the *Y* in USE YOUR VOTE! and stood back, paintbrush dripping black paint on the grass, to get the full effect.

"We can't spare a day just so you can march. We're a week and a half behind schedule now. At least."

"Helping the cause of women's suffrage is one of the reasons for this walk, too," she said as she turned to me. "It's our duty to march and remind the women of Utah that the right to vote they won last year isn't any good unless they use it."

Two weeks after the lava fields, Ma was still gaunt and I didn't know how she could stir the energy to do any walking she didn't have to do. I couldn't talk her out of marching, but I did talk her into letting me carry the sign for her. We fell into line behind the fife and drum marching unit, and I obediently emulated her smart marching style and waved the sign.

CHAPTER 14

I TAKE A TUMBLE

July 8, 1896–Day 64

Salt Lake City, Utah

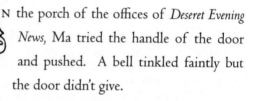

ON the porch of the offices of *Deseret Evening News,* Ma tried the handle of the door and pushed. A bell tinkled faintly but the door didn't give.

I pointed to the sign in the window of the door. "They're closed, Ma," I said, and turned to go away.

"You always give up too easily," Ma said in that lecturing tone that made me clench my teeth. "They might be closed to ordinary people, but they'll want our story."

I had been walking since dawn with nothing but a crust of bread for breakfast. Sweat pooled down my rib cage under my armpits, and yet I was willing to walk another twenty-five miles for all the tomorrows until we reached New York. I dropped my satchel. "I do not always give up too easily! If I did, I'd already be back in Mica Creek instead of being nibbled to pieces by mosquitoes and wearing my feet off to the kneecaps."

Ma smiled at my outburst and conceded. "Well, maybe not always. But I still bet there are people in there; they just don't want anyone interrupting their lunch." She cupped her hands around her eyes to peer into the window. She straightened, full of herself because she was right. "There is somebody back there," she said. "See for yourself."

I obediently put my face close enough to the glass to leave a nose print on it. *Uff da!* A shadowy figure strode toward the door. I back-stepped twice and—catching my heel on the edge of the sidewalk—toppled backwards, seat-first, into the street, my feet propped up on the sidewalk and skirts halfway up to my knees.

The door opened and a young man—unsuccessfully suppressing laughter—crossed the sidewalk to give me a hand up. "It's not funny," I said.

"Sorry," he said. "But if you'd seen the outraged look on your face when you lost your balance, you'd have laughed, too." His grin faded as he held my hand a little longer than he had to while he examined my face. "You're not hurt, are you?"

"I'm fine," I said, brushing off my skirt to avoid meeting his eyes again.

"Here," he said heartily as he retrieved my hat from the gutter. "Looks like your hat was the only casualty." He held it out toward me. His thumb and forefinger were stained with ink just where a pen would rest.

That poor hat. It was the cheapest one I could find. Within days it had started to unravel, and with loose ends of straw poking out helter-skelter, it had made me look like I had just crawled out from under a haystack. "Believe it or not, it looked that bad before I fell," I said.

Ma wasn't used to my having the reporter's attention. "Young man," she said, putting herself in his range of vision, "I'd like to talk to the features editor."

"Do you have a story?" He opened the door wider and escorted us in with a bow.

He introduced himself as he closed the door. "I'm Charles Doré." He said his name the French way: "Shahrl Doray."

Ma handed him one of her *cartes de visite.* "We've walked clear from Spokane and we're headed to New York City. I'm Helga Estby."

Before I could introduce myself, Mr. Doré looked up from Ma's card. "And you must be 'and daughter'?"

"Yes," I said. My cheeks burned. I hated always being "and daughter." I hated my luck—meeting the first reporter near my age while nearly upside down, my posterior in the street, and soot-stained petticoats in full view.

As he led us back toward a cluster of desks, I fanned myself with a blank piece of paper I had picked up from one of the desks. In spite of the heat, Mr. Doré pulled on a seersucker jacket that had been draped across the back of his chair. As he leaned over to pull chairs from the adjacent desks closer to his desk, I caught a whiff of Pears soap. I had not washed my hair in a month and had had only two tub baths since Mica Creek.

As I settled into the chair, I casually shifted one hand to cover the place I'd ripped my skirt on barbed wire. If my guardian angel wasn't busy saving someone's life, I hoped she could keep Mr. Doré from noticing the bug bites on my cheeks, the black crescents of grime rimming my cuticles, and my frayed hems blackened with dirt.

While Mr. Doré was taking notes, I gradually worked my hands out of sight in the folds of my skirt and tucked my feet back under the chair to hide my men's secondhand work boots.

After sixty performances of her standard talk, Ma could still get her voice to tremble movingly when she got to the part in her talk about the imminent loss of our farm. My ears pricked when she started a melodramatic account of the time I shot a man in Oregon.

I nudged Ma's shin, but she kept talking.

I interrupted. "Don't put that part in, Mr. Doré. I—I'm not really...it was the first time I ever shot anyone, and then it was only in the leg—not that I intend to shoot anyone else...oh, *uff da*." Anyone who had grown up with Norwegians would know that there are two ways *uff da* can be said. One is at full volume, with gusto, usually uttered to take the place of an expression unacceptable to one's catechism teacher or maiden aunt. The other is softly, resignedly, with a sigh.

I held my breath while I watched Mr. Doré to see if he was impressed, amused, or shocked. "Since you're carrying a gun," he said, "I guess I better be on good behavior." His tone was solemn, but his mouth twitched toward another grin. When he looked down at his notebook again, I guided a strand of haystack-brown hair back into my bun and tried to scrape off some of the loose, peeling flakes on my chapped lips with my teeth, but even these slight movements drew his eyes back to my face and I could feel my rough cheeks grow hotter yet.

Ma gave Mr. Doré the details of our appearance tomorrow, when we would be modeling the new bicycle costumes and presenting a lecture on our travels.

Since I was curious about what he was writing about us, I stood and tiptoed around to the back of his desk and looked over his shoulder. Mr. Doré stopped writing and turned over his notepad. "You'll blush if you see what I've written," he said. "Or are you admiring my typewriter? I had to save for six months to buy it—it's a Model Two Underwood."

As he stood, he pulled down his sleeves to cover his wrists. If I were Sherlock Holmes I'd have said that jacket used to belong to someone else, or Mr. Reporter had grown since he bought it and couldn't afford to replace it. And yet he had found money to buy a new typewriter. I had to admire his determination to keep up with the times.

"Pretty soon publishers won't be accepting manuscripts in longhand. I ought to know — I've already published three short stories. One in *Scribner's* — 'Latecomer's Lament' — did you see it?" He paused expectantly.

I shrugged apologetically and shook my head.

"Well," he said. He reached down to use the back of one sleeve to wipe a fleck of dust off the front, where *Underwood* shone in gold letters.

When he straightened, it struck me that I was exactly his height, so his eyes looked directly into mine. His green eyes, flecked with gold, looked owlish behind gold round-rimmed glasses. "I sure wish I was seeing the country like you and your mother," he said. "All the interesting people you'd meet — I'd have material for a million stories with a trip like that."

I laughed. "You'd also have to like walking for days without ever getting dry, being eaten by mosquitoes, and wondering when you'd eat next."

"But that's part of the adventure, isn't it?"

"Easy to say when you work at a desk and go home to dinner and a warm bed every night," I said. "I'm going to write, too," I said, daring him to say I was only a farm girl off on a lark with my mother and had no chance in the world of writing anything someone would want to read.

"Going to write isn't the same as writing," he said. He used the same lecturing tone Ma used, but from him it didn't rankle. It was good advice, even if it was coming from someone who didn't look more than a few years older than I was.

Ma looked at the clock on the wall. "Enough dawdling," she said as she picked up her satchel and tugged me toward the door. "Time we made it to the dressmaker's."

"Hey," he said as we headed out. "Would you like a couple souvenir pencils?"

They were Eberhard Fabers, embossed with "Deseret Evening News" in blue letters on one side.

"Thanks," I said.

We were halfway down the block when he called after us. "See you tomorrow!"

I turned to wave. The sun had caught his hair, turning it to incandescent copper.

We walked up one flight of stairs and toward the south end of the arcade to Miss Lulu Jones's shop. With good reason, she was reluctant to have us try on our new clothes before we had bathed, so she led us to her nearby apartment, where we both bathed and washed our hair. I was mortified at the black ring I left in her tub.

After braiding each other's damp hair, we walked back to the shop, where we changed into the bicycle costumes we would model tomorrow. In the dressing room, I ran my rough fingers over the Pluette storm serge of the midcalf skirt. According to the tag, it was the same smooth, tightly woven wool used in English ladies' riding habits. I took off my battered hat, which I planned to feed to the first goat I saw. In its place, I set a crisp straw boater with a black grosgrain ribbon hatband. Looking in the mirror, I was pleased. No frippery, just well-tailored simplicity. Fine-knit stockings with no holes, new chemise and shorter petticoat, kid boots instead of men's work shoes. It was the very thing Jo March would have chosen to wear if *Little Women* had been set in today's time instead of the Civil War. It was the very thing Nellie Bly would wear to interview the president. It was exactly what I wished I had been wearing when I had met Mr. Doré.

I stepped back from the mirror. If I squinted, the mosquito bites were hardly noticeable. I tried fluttering my eyelashes like my sister Ida, but I just looked like I had a train cinder in my eye.

Friday, July 10 – Day 66
Salt Lake City, Utah

By noon I was too faint to eat. My serge jacket looked smart, but it was too hot for this weather. I patted the film of moisture from my forehead and wiped my palms on my handkerchief to avoid spoiling my skirt.

I scanned the audience for Mr. Doré's face as I reluctantly mounted the steps to the stage. Miss Jones introduced us as "those valiant women walkers" and Ma explained anew why she felt this was her last chance to save the farm and prove that women were intelligent, resourceful, and deserved the vote in every state, following Utah's good example.

Once her own agenda was satisfied, she launched enthusiastically into her endorsement for clothing developed for the New Woman. She described how much she would have appreciated walking in shorter bicycle skirts that were inches above the mud. She praised the new Ferris Bicycle Corset and Nazareth Waists with elastic strips that allowed a woman to get a full breath. She could have been a revival preacher or Lydia Pinkham's tonic salesman.

My attention was diverted from Ma when Mr. Doré whooshed in from one of the side streets and leaned his bicycle against a building. He raised his notebook in a salute. I watched—trying not to look as if I were watching—as he sidled through the standing listeners to a point directly in front of me.

Mr. Doré wrote down Ma's answers to each question from the audience. Each time he looked expectantly toward me, waiting for me to say something, I had to look away. I had complained about Ma getting all the credit for this walk, but now, with a chance to get some notice, I hoped I could avoid opening my mouth.

Finally, a young woman directed a question my way and I had to speak: "Miss Estby, what did you pack to take with you?"

I inhaled as deeply as my corset would allow and flicked my eyes toward Mr. Doré, who smiled encouragingly and held his notebook and pencil at the ready.

"Well," I said, "I packed emergency things first, like a first-aid kit, canteen, and matches. Pa thought we should take a gun with us, so I packed a pistol and bullets." I swallowed as I remembered the scratch of Pa's mustache on my cheek as he leaned low behind me to show me how to line up the sights and squeeze the trigger.

"Pa taught me how to shoot," I said. "And my brother Arthur helped me practice." Mr. Doré wrote down a word or two on his notepad and looked up to see what I would say next. My mind was an untidy storeroom with facts jumbled together in no logical order. Pa's teaching me to shoot was not even what she asked about. Oh, *ish da, ish da!*

Ma apparently couldn't stand my dithering and gave up the struggle to keep silent. "We compared our lists of what each would take and packed very scientifically." She succinctly listed what each of us had packed, making it sound like she was the organized one. I noticed a few gasps from women in the audience when she said we didn't have room in our satchels for a change of clothes.

Finally Ma stopped talking and Miss Jones stood to thank us and to let everyone know that everything we were wearing had come from the shops right there in the Brooks Arcade.

A group of women greeted us at the bottom of the stairs

to get Ma's autograph and ask more questions. Ma glowed with all the attention.

I was gratified to have three or four women ask me for my autograph, although one of the women held her autograph book and pen toward me gingerly, as if she wanted my autograph but not the vermin I might be harboring after two months on the road.

After everyone in the audience had drifted away to look at the bicycles on display or investigate the shops, Mr. Doré approached us. "You had quite a turnout," he said.

"After they found out they wouldn't get clean clothes every day, there wasn't a one who would join us, though," I said.

"I'd join you if I could."

Perhaps daydreaming of the open road, he flushed, then sighed and put his notepad and pencil in his jacket pocket. "So," he said, turning to Ma and nodding toward his shiny black bicycle, "would you like to try out your bicycle skirt on my new Columbia?" He asked Ma, but his smile strayed back to my face as he spoke.

Ma tucked another handful of change she'd raised by selling *cartes de visite* with our pictures on them into her satchel before she spoke. "I'm too old to make a fool of myself in front of all these people," she said. (If he believed that, he was not as smart as he looked.) "Let Clara try." She put one hand on her hip and shook her head as I followed Mr. Doré toward his bicycle.

I had observed other people riding bicycles and feigned confidence as I lifted my skirts to swing my right leg over the bar, perch on the seat, and position my feet on the pedals.

"It's easier if you start with the right pedal up," Mr. Doré said, and supported the bicycle with one hand over mine on the handlebars and the other, alarmingly, on the back of the very bicycle seat I occupied. He pushed gently until the right pedal rotated to the top. "Pump! Right foot down."

I pushed down, and the bicycle wobbled forward.

"It's like jumping off the shed roof," he said. "You can't do it slowly. Build up speed and you won't wobble."

I was terrified, but willing to jump off the top of the highest barn roof into a burning haystack if it would improve Mr. Doré's opinion of me. I pumped furiously, and by some magic I did not fall. I could hear his breathing as he ran along beside me, ready to save his bicycle if I faltered.

As we approached a four-story brick building that blocked the end of the street, he said with surprising calm, "Turn the handlebars now, and slow down."

"Which way?" I said. My voice was not calm.

"Either, just do it!"

I jerked the handlebars first one way, then the other in indecision and stopped pedaling in a panic. Only Mr. Doré's good reflexes prevented my momentum from crashing my face into the brick wall and getting more than the tiniest nick on the front fender of Mr. Doré's new Columbia bicycle. As his hands darted out to catch the bicycle, our heads bumped and I felt his cheek brush mine. I swung off the seat, not taking time to think that by swinging off on the left I would be very nearly occupying the same space as Mr. Doré. For an instant, we stood barely an inch apart before I stepped awkwardly backward.

Mr. Doré grinned, and I noticed for the first time that his incisors were slightly slanted into a space too small for them. "How was your ride, Miss Estby?" he said.

I looked straight into his gold-flecked eyes and matched my grin to his. "Brilliant," I said.

CHAPTER 15

I WRITE

July 13–Day 69
Utah, on the way to Wyoming

A s WE backtracked to Ogden to where the Union Pacific track headed east through the Wasatch Range, I imagined what it would be like to ride a bicycle instead of walking across the plains ahead. I would pedal so fast, I'd create my own wind. I'd suck in air in hungry gusts as my hair streamed out behind. The miles would fall behind me as in a dream.

As long as I was imagining, I wondered what it would be like to have Mr. Doré on a bicycle beside me. Would we laugh together as a hare darted back and forth across our trail, then pretended to hide behind a bush before darting out to race us again? Would we be content to watch the rising sun in silence as we pedaled eastward, or would he need to offer a steady commentary on it, like Ma?

I tried to remember and decode his every word and gesture. Had he let me ride his bicycle because he thought I was a child to be amused? Or had he used his bicycle as an excuse to be near me? Had his cheek brushed mine by accident? Or on purpose?

At least once an hour I twirled, admiring the graceful swirl of my shorter gored skirt. Was the lightness I felt from less fabric around the ankles, or my skin's memory of his touch?

I tried to remember Erick Iverson's face. Although I had known him since I was ten years old, all I could bring to mind was a bland oval face with thinning fair hair, bowl cut by his sister Alma. He was just one of the Iverson brothers: too loud, all elbows and big feet; a good farmer with curiosity limited to soil, grain types, insects that damaged grains, farm equipment, and weather. The thought of him did not make my chest swell like a bellows. The thought of him did not put a Mona Lisa smile on my face. Not like Charles.

Silently I said his Christian name the French way, as he did. *Shahrl.* My mouth puckered halfway to a kiss to pronounce the soft *Ch*. In the imaginings that made the time flow faster than a river after rain, he was always Charles, and I was his Clara.

July 18, 1896 – Day 74

Wyoming

~e⌒e~

Dear Mr. Doré,

My mother and I neglected to tell you the particulars of our schedule for the remainder of our journey. Should you need to contact us for details of subsequent portions of our travels, please send a letter care of general delivery in the following cities where we will check for mail on approximately these dates:

Denver—September 1

Omaha—October 1

Chicago—October 25

Pittsburgh—November 9

New York—November 30 (We may have a five-day
        extension to December 5.)

To prove that I have been following your advice to write, not just talk about writing, I have also enclosed an account of our encounter with the Ute Indians, which may be of interest to your readers. If your paper publishes my account, would you send me a copy?

Sincerely,
Miss Clara Estby

P.S. I hope you were able to repair the scratch I put on your bicycle fender when I wobbled into the bricks on the wall of the arcade.

P.P.S. Ma had a chance to trade me to a Ute brave for three horses, but she decided to keep me.

P.P.P.S. I wrote the story with the Deseret Evening News pencil you gave me.

Women Walkers among the Indians
Being a first-person account of a
peaceful encounter with the Indians of Utah
Submitted by Clara Estby, transcontinental pedestrian

By the time we reached Utah, Ma and I had been walking over two months and covered nine hundred and eleven miles. I had already worn out four pairs of shoes. Unfortunately, I had only one pair of feet, and they had to last me until New York City.

One day in mid-July, midway between Ogden and the border to Wyoming, I had the feeling Ma and I were not alone. As I slowly scanned the horizon for anything alive in all those lonesome miles of stone and sagebrush, my eye caught movement to the left. Three long-haired men on horseback galloped from behind a tall red butte a dozen yards out and reined to a stop so close to us that we could count the whiskers on each horse's muzzle.

I was no stranger to Indians. My mother and I had crossed the entire Umatilla Reservation on foot. But on the reservation we were never far from help. Here we had passed no settlement, white or Indian, for miles, and who knew what these braves intended? One Indian said something in his ancient language and rode away to the southeast. When the other two slid from their horses and grabbed my mother and me by our hands, my throat hurt from holding back a scream.

What were they trying to tell us? They gestured repeatedly in the direction their leader had ridden, then remounted and gestured again, urging us to follow them. If they had meant us harm, they would have tied us up and thrown us over their saddles; since they had left us free to walk on our own, dared we to think their motives were good?

"What do you think, Clara?" Ma asked.

"I don't think we have much choice," I said. "We can't outrun their horses. Let's hope your guardian angel is looking out for us today."

Like addle-headed, reluctant sheep, we let ourselves be herded, with great trepidation. After less than an hour, we reached their camp of seven huts made of brush over sapling frames. The two Indians slid off their horses and nudged us toward a cluster of women and children. As I inhaled the aroma of roasting meat, I was reminded that Ma and I hadn't eaten since breakfast, at least twenty-five miles of walking ago. I hoped they'd share.

One small girl summoned the courage to leave her mother's side and approach me. At first she just stared, one finger in her mouth, glints of firelight in her dark eyes. Such a little Indian, not much older than my little sister Lillian at home, was not frightening. I started breathing normally again as I knelt beside her. "Hello," I whispered. "My name is Clara."

After looking toward her mother for reassurance, the girl touched my bangs, which I'd turned in tight corkscrews that morning with my mother's curling iron. My stomach rumbled. Would a demonstration of the iron be sufficient trade for dinner?

Ma stood over us, smiling down at the child's curiosity. I looked up. "Ma, do you think they'd like to see your curling iron?"

She opened her bag to find her iron, and handed it to the woman who appeared to be the mother of the little girl. At the sight of the iron, several men drifted closer to take a look. Soon Ma's curling iron was making a circuit around the campfire. As it was passed from hand to hand for inspection, one boy used it as a toy gun. An older man put his finger in the space meant for a lock of hair and closed the clamp. He opened and shut the clamp again, trying to fathom its use. Then he passed it on.

When the iron reached my mother, she caught a loose strand of her hair and wound it until it was close to the scalp. When she released the strand, the hair fell straight. The Indians were not impressed. For a real demonstration the iron would have to be hot.

She ceremoniously approached the fire, holding the curling iron in front of her in outstretched hands like a consecrated offering. She kneeled to place the rod near the edge of the fire and stood as she waited for the iron to heat. When she leaned over the fire and spit lightly on the curling iron, the bead of water sizzled and evaporated immediately; the iron was ready. She picked up the curling iron by the wood handle and drew it slowly back and forth in front of her, as if to bless — or cast a spell on — the crowd of Indians watching her. She summoned me to her.

A laugh bubbled in my chest, but I didn't want to spoil her solemn ritual, so I fought off my smile as *she selected a strand of hair from the side of my face. She placed her left hand between the rod and my face as she rolled my hair, like she had when I was a child, making sure that if I fidgeted, the hot iron would burn her fingers and not my cheek. Looking sideways, I saw her hands just an inch away. At home she had pushed back her cuticles and rubbed in lotion every night. Now her nails were ragged, and windblown grit had tattooed fine lines in the folds across each knuckle.*

She eased the rod from the coil of my hair and stood back so everyone could see the straw-colored corkscrew dangling along my cheek. While the iron was still hot, she made a matching ringlet on the other side of my face. I held my arms slightly away from my body and turned slowly in the firelight, like a mannequin, so everyone could see. I closed my eyes, feeling the heat of the fire first on one side, then the other.

My mother was in great demand as a hairstylist for the rest of the evening, as women, children, and even a man or two lined up for curls in her fireside salon. The Indians I had been so afraid of two hours ago shared their food and fire with us. I wondered how long those three men had followed us earlier in the day before deciding we might appreciate their help.

Just before sealing the story into an envelope addressed to Mr. Doré, I decided the story wasn't good enough and wrote a new letter with just our schedule. The next day I decided that if I couldn't get my story published where I knew someone, I'd never get it published anywhere, so I revised, re-revised, and re-re-revised. After two more days, erasing and changing until I wore holes in the paper and my *Deseret Evening News* pencil was worn down to the eraser, I finally sealed the story into an envelope and mailed it to Mr. Doré. I kept a near-final draft for myself, and copied a slightly shorter version of it in my letter to Arthur, Johnny, and William.

Three months ago, who could have imagined me — boring Clara — camping out with Indians in Utah! Even if I spent the rest of my life back in Mica Creek, I'd have memories like that night to remind me of the world outside a patch of wheat. Besides saving the farm, was that what Ma was looking for on this trip, too? For both of us?

CHAPTER 16

SOMEONE TO LISTEN

July 20, 1896–Day 76

Somewhere in Wyoming

I WAS lonesome for company besides Ma, so I trod the miles imagining soulful conversations with Mr. Doré. He would ask me what prompted me to strike out on this adventure and I would quote Walt Whitman's lines from "Song of the Open Road": "Afoot and light-hearted, I take to the open road, / Healthy, free, the world before me..." He would say, "Why, Whitman is my favorite poet!" and ask me if I knew that Whitman was a newsman, too.

Next, he would say I reminded him of Nellie Bly, girl reporter for the *New York World*. I would blush becomingly at the comparison. He would say, "We are truly kindred spirits," and I would agree that indeed we were.

July 21, 1896 – Day 77
Still nowhere, Wyoming

More lonesome walking through miles of flat scrub. Counted three dead porcupines on the tracks. When I left the trail to see what ravens were squabbling about in the brush I discovered a hoofed leg protruding from a pile of dirt, loose fur, and twigs. As I turned back to rejoin Ma, I almost stepped in a pile of fly-crusted, coiled innards, then lost my breakfast. *Ish da.*

"Are you all right, Clara?" Ma asked as she walked toward me.

"Just ravens cleaning up after a cougar, Ma." I took a sip of water from my canteen, swished, and spit to wash away the sour taste in my mouth. Cougars didn't like the intestines, so as soon as they bit off the belly fur and ripped open the undersides of their prey, they dragged out the intestines and piled them up out of the way so they could get at the liver. I thought about a cougar piling up my intestines for the ravens, and wondered if human liver tasted as good to them as a deer's.

We had already been carrying sticks to clear our path of snakes, but we had another reason to feel safer with stout sticks now. Between looking up at every ledge and overhanging tree limb for cougars and down around every rock for rattlers, it was a wonder I ever kept track of my feet.

We didn't pass any homesteads this whole day, so we had to sleep outside. A spindly tree didn't offer real protection against cougars, snakes, or rain, but I still preferred to sleep cozied under a pine rather than in the open scrub. We spread our ponchos over mounded brush and stretched out, alert to the sounds of the night. Every mouse scurry became a rattlesnake; every lonesome coyote howl became the vanguard of a hungry wolf pack. I finally slept—backside up, to protect my innards.

July 27, 1896 – Day 83
Between nowhere and more nowhere, Wyoming

Nothing to report this week except that, in spite of having to stop for Ma to rest more often, we kept to our goal of twenty-five miles a day. I entertained myself by watching dust devils and the shifting shadows on the ground cast from clouds above, and by convincing myself that over the next rise I would discover something wondrous. It was always more miles of scrub.

Other than the occasional passing train, it was like Ma and I were the last people left on the planet.

July 30, 1896 – Day 86
Approaching civilization in Rawlins, Wyoming

Ma was even quieter today, smaller and wilted. I tried to perk her up with some "do you remembers," but she said she was too thirsty to talk. I couldn't let her slip into a down spell so far from home. Would new people to talk to put her starch back? I was as ruthless as Simon Legree in *Uncle Tom's Cabin*. Pushing her to walk an extra fifteen miles today—forty total—we reached Rawlins, the first place bigger than a whistle stop in one hundred and twenty miles. We checked in at the *Carbon County Journal* office and gave our story. The publisher, Mr. Friend, said he knew someone who would likely take us in tonight.

We walked out West Cedar Street to a boxy two-story house with flowered curtains in the window and knocked. The woman who opened the door was not much taller than my sister Ida, and dressed as elegantly as Ida did in her dreams. "I'm Dr. Holmes," she said with a smile, and invited us in.

I was relieved to see Ma brighten at a new face. She started talking almost faster than a body's ears could listen. Mercifully, I did not have to listen to her "why women should have the right to vote" talk again, since women had voted in Wyoming since just after the Civil War. Dr. Holmes was a champion listener.

By ten o'clock I was yawning, but Ma was still wearing a path in the rug describing—with exuberant hand gestures as well as words—Henry's death, her bout with consumption, her previous plans to save the farm, and how she was sure this walk across the country was the best idea she'd ever had. "I had to do something. I couldn't stay put and let the farm go to the sheriff's sale." Ma looked at me.

"You're right, Ma," I said. "We had to do something." At

the thought of another four months to go, however, I wondered if this walk had been the right something.

Without saying another word, Ma got out her journal and began to write, as if she were alone in the room.

Dr. Holmes smiled toward me. "Want to find a breeze on the porch?"

I followed her outside and sat on the edge of the porch, leaning against one of the pillars. Dr. Holmes and I looked at the stars in friendly silence for several minutes. Then she spoke. "Your mother must have an iron constitution if she can have consumption one month and start to walk across the country the next. I never had a patient who could do that."

"You never know about Ma," I said. "For months she'll hardly sleep and wear everyone out with her projects and then she'll need to sleep a lot. After Henry died, she did have a cough, and although she said it was consumption, I thought she was just being melodramatic, or using consumption as an excuse to work through her dismals in bed. When she got up, she was in another of her whirlwind moods. She had more endurance than I did when we left Mica Creek. But she's slowing down now. I hope she can make it to New York City."

"I think you may be right—that your mother was just sad, not sick. It sounds like she just needed an excuse to stay in bed until she was ready to face the world. This walk across the country gave her a reason to get up. You say your mother has taken to bed before?" Dr. Holmes asked.

"Three times that I remember. The longest time—nearly two years—was when she fell on sidewalk the city had broken up, getting ready for repairs. She fractured her pelvis and couldn't walk again until she got the city to pay for an operation. I took over for her all of seventh and eighth grades."

Dr. Holmes shifted to lean against the other pillar. "How did you manage?"

"I stayed home from school so I could take care of Ma and the younger ones, but my school-age brothers and sisters brought my assignments home so I could study after dinner. I not only graduated from eighth grade with my class, but with first-place marks. Ma was so proud of me, she talked Pa into letting me hire out to one of her suffrage society friends in Spokane so I'd have a place to live while I went to high school in town. I was a servant, but at least I got to go on to school."

Other than the sounds of someone pumping water into a tin pail nearby, crickets, and two dogs having a conversation, the night was quiet.

"It sounds like you've been so busy taking care of everybody else that you haven't had time to think about what you want to do for yourself." Dr. Holmes patted my shoulder. "Your ma is lucky to have you, but don't let her ups and downs keep you from living your own life forever. While you're on this sabbatical, think about what you want to do next."

"I know what I want to do—write. But I also like to eat." I turned to face Dr. Holmes. "More than the farm is at stake in this walk. If we win the money, I can go to college and study writing. If we lose, I stay in Mica Creek and marry the boy next door." I slumped back against the pillar.

When she put a hand on my shoulder I straightened up again with a start.

"How can a smart young woman like you leave one of the most important decisions you'll ever make up to fate? Don't you know your own mind? You don't strike me as a young woman who would be content with Mica Creek and the world she can see from her front porch. Your ma isn't, and you must take after her."

I shook my shoulder free from her hand. "You're the first person besides Ma who ever said I was a bit like her. Most people say I'm more like my Pa." I fingered Pa's owl in my pocket. "I wish I knew for sure I could make it as a writer. Then I could stop dithering about my future and write."

Dr. Holmes leaned forward and took both my hands. "Sometimes you just have to try something and see if it works. I taught school for a year or so, and then apprenticed myself to a doctor for another year before I decided to go to medical school. I can give you one inflexible piece of advice." She made sure I was looking at her before she continued. "Don't marry to avoid making up your mind about what else to do. And learn skills to support yourself before you do anything else. One reason young men have more choices in their lives is that..."

"They don't have babies," I finished.

"Yes, that too," she said. "But what I meant to say is that men make better wages than women, so it's easier for them to save money for college. Domestic work, teaching, nursing —none of the traditional women's work pays a hill of beans. Learn to do something men get paid well for."

I withdrew my hands and held up one arm to test my muscle. "Do you know a blacksmith who needs an apprentice?"

Dr. Holmes laughed. "I was thinking of something that favored brain over brawn, but with such formidable biceps, blacksmithing might be a possibility."

Ma was asleep in the guest room when Dr. Holmes and I went back into the house. In five minutes I was beside Ma in bed, but thinking through Dr. Holmes's advice kept me awake. Ma had said I might be more like her than I thought. Now Dr. Holmes thought I favored Ma, too! What similarity between Ma and me did she see that I couldn't? We didn't have anything but our front teeth in common. She could out-talk the hawker of magic elixir, and I ran out of things to say once I stammered hello. Ma thrived on attention, being different, marching with the suffragists, tromping clear across the country, and getting her picture in the *New York World*. I would do anything to avoid attention. Her notions had her blooming fiery orange like her Austrian Copper rose, then going dormant as a stick. I was more like a pine tree, never blooming—just a steady, predictable green.

I did agree with Dr. Holmes on one thing, though. I wasn't going to let the outcome of this walk decide whether or not I would marry Erick. If I didn't want to marry Erick I wouldn't. I just had to sit down and write a letter to tell him so.

*To: Miss A. J. Waterson, 95 William Street,
      New York City, New York*

From: Helga Estby

Monthly report # 3: Fort Fred Steele, Wyoming

Miles covered, July 4—August 4: 424

*Notes: Peaceful encounter with Ute Indians. Let us know as
soon as possible if our previous request for extension of time
due to heat stroke in the lava fields is granted.*

CHAPTER 17

WE BATTLE NATURE

August 10, 1896–Day 97

Wyoming

E were climbing into the Medicine Bow Mountains at the pace of slugs. We should have been on the far side of Nebraska by now. If Ma hadn't had to wait for the governor's signature in Boise, if she hadn't insisted on that shortcut across the lava fields, if she hadn't felt the weight of the entire suffrage movement on her shoulders and wasted a day in Ogden marching with her sign...if, if, if.

Every time I thought of how far behind we were getting I wanted to howl.

Ma would never have made it this far without me, yet it hadn't occurred to her to put my name on her *cartes de visite*. I was just "and daughter" like something else she had packed in her satchel and brought out in emergencies. Need someone shot? Need someone to drag you through the lava fields? Whip out your trusty Clara; she'll take care of it.

By the point where the tracks entered a narrow gorge, I waited for Ma to catch up. I sighed impatiently when she stopped again, smiling at the wildflowers and taking in the mountains, a backdrop for some nameless lake.

"No lollygagging!" I called out.

"Of course you're spry; you didn't have consumption all winter." Her chest rose and fell with the effort of walking uphill; maybe she wasn't lollygagging but had to rest.

"I always said you didn't have consumption, and Dr. Holmes agreed with me," I called out.

"How would she know? She wasn't in Mica Creek when I was sick."

"Humph. She said you were sad, not sick," I said.

When Ma caught up with me, she put down her satchel so she could gesture freely—one hand on her hip, one finger pointing to the middle button on my sweat-stained shirtwaist. "You don't understand what real sadness is like. After Henry died, you bustled on through your chores every single day like nothing happened. I feel things more strongly than you do."

"I feel things every bit as strongly as you do. I just don't wallow in those feelings. You have to steel yourself to do what needs doing."

Ma shook her head. "It goes beyond sad. I don't know if there's even a word for it."

"Melancholy, depths of despair, despondency?"

"Stronger yet. It's more like—like an elephant sitting on your chest. No amount of willpower is going to make that elephant move. You just have to suffer until the elephant takes a mind to get up and leave you alone for a while. But you know he'll be back. And you won't be able to do anything about it the next time, either, except wait for him to go away."

"The trouble is, when your elephant comes to call, I have to take over for you. And besides those times you can't help, there are all those times you trot to Spokane to sip tea and talk votes." When I realized I was standing with one hand on my hip and one finger pointing at Ma—mirroring her pose—I jerked my arms down to my sides.

"And another thing," I said. "You would never make it on your own to New York, but I let you get all the attention in the interviews, since getting your name in the papers seems to be as important to you as winning the bet. I didn't even complain about not getting my name on your hoity-toity *cartes de visite*."

Ma huffed. "You don't want to talk to the reporters, anyway. Unless," she added, "they're under thirty and let you ride their bicycles." She smiled, trying to coax a smile from me.

I turned my back on Ma and headed on up the tracks into the gorge.

Ma followed, continuing her side of the argument. "You wouldn't have made it on your own, either. I have had to talk us into a bed and a meal every night. If it weren't for me you would have starved to death by now. Anyway, I should have my name on the cards. It was my idea for the walk."

I stopped and whirled. "I gave you the idea!" My voice squeaked in indignation. "I was talking about Nellie Bly and her trip around the world and that's when you said you'd see if you could find someone to pay you to walk."

By now there was no longer room for us to walk side by side, so I crossed the tracks to find space for my feet on the other side.

"But you didn't do anything with your idea, did you?" Ma said. She looked up from treacherous footing in the broken rock long enough to shoot me an accusing glance.

I had to admit to myself that I hadn't.

"And if it weren't for me, you'd still be back in Mica Creek, marrying Erick because you didn't have the gumption to tell him no outright and figure out what you wanted to do with your life. I'm trying to teach you some gumption and you just whine about not getting your name on the cards."

"But..."

"Listen here, Clara Estby. Show some respect to your mother."

"How about showing some respect to me? Didn't it occur to you I might be right about not taking the shortcut in Idaho?"

Ma stopped, dropped her arms, and looked to heaven for forbearance. I followed her glance upward. The clouds were dark now, and scudding fast.

"I knew you wouldn't let me forget that. You've just been stewing on that for a thousand miles until you couldn't stand it anymore. We all make mistakes. And anyone with an ounce of curiosity or courage knows that making mistakes is better than living in a padded room your whole life, afraid to try anything new."

I shivered as the wind picked up and whipped through the trees. "Who are you to give me advice? I'd never throw away my future by having a child at fifteen and sentencing myself to a life like yours."

At Ma's shocked expression, I almost slapped my hands over my mouth. I shouldn't have said that. What's more, I hadn't just said it; I had yelled it to be heard over the wind, which had picked up from a pleasant breeze to a yowling gale.

"I'm sorry..." I started, then held my breath when the wind halted abruptly. The air felt heavy. The birds went silent. The hair on my arms rose with a tickle. Then — *crack!* — the sky lit up and thunder exploded almost beside us. Lightning flashed again with simultaneous thunder like a gunshot. Barely thirty feet away, atop a crag on one side of the channel cut for the tracks, a tree split open and began to burn.

We looked right into lightning bolts flashing on every side. Thunder bounced off rock walls on either side of us, and the echoes made it impossible to tell which rolls of thunder went with which flashes. Thunder rattled my rib cage and set my eardrums ringing. Thunder mocked the puny anger I'd let loose on Ma.

"Lie down!" she yelled as she threw herself down as far from the tracks as the narrow passage between walls of rock allowed.

I continued to stand, clenching my carved owl in my pocket. Cinders floated around us like snow. The wind roared through the pass again, blowing fire and cinders uphill beyond us and sweeping in a fresh bank of clouds. The wind shrieked through the trees above us, bending them, breaking them. The wind could have picked me up like a dry leaf and blown me to the next county. As the clouds were pushed higher up the side of the mountain, they loosed their water, dousing the fire and drenching us. To stand against the wind as I struggled into my poncho, I imagined my feet sending down strong tap roots to anchor me to the rock.

Rain fell by the wagonload. Water cascaded down the rocky slopes in waterfalls that created a stream that swept first over my toes, then ankles, my shins, and over my boots. We had walls of sheer blasted rock on either side. There was no escape.

After Ma pulled on her rain gear, we waded haltingly against the current, encumbered by water-weighted skirts. With wind roaring up through the pass and water rushing down, I felt like I was being stretched between two horses galloping in opposite directions. I gripped my satchel and reached out to one side of the canyon walls to steady myself against the racing river. Who would believe we could drown in the mountains? Five minutes ago I had been worried about not getting to New

York by the end of November. Now I just wanted to stay alive until tomorrow.

Rain and spray blurred my vision, but I made out Ma's meaning as she jabbed her chin to the right. Twenty-five feet beyond us, a shallow, two-foot-wide channel in the rock sloped up like a water-swept grain chute leading to a ledge above the torrent. If we could reach that ledge, we might survive.

I grabbed a bush to steady myself against the power of the water, but the bush broke away with a jerk. I stumbled backward, touching bottom with my seat as my poncho floated like a lily pad around me. Ma heard my yelp above the roar of the water and turned to help me stand. Holding hands, we pushed together against the rising water toward the base of the upward channel.

I put the rope handle of my satchel over my shoulder and shifted it to rest on the back of my hip. Water cascading down the chute made it feel like I was climbing a river to get to the ledge. I clutched at small slippery knobs of rock with my right hand and braced my left forearm against the other side of the channel. For the first few footholds, I felt Ma's hands guiding my boots. Then she shouted something, which I couldn't hear clearly over the rumbling thunder and tumbling water. She shouted again, "I'm sorry, Clara!"

I searched for her hand with my foot, but there was nothing but air. Was she sorry she could not reach my feet to help me? Was she sorry we had ever left Mica Creek? I searched blindly for places to brace my feet and knees and clambered up the last few feet.

Fifteen feet above the new river, the chute leveled out and I pushed myself onto the ledge and looked down. "I made it, Ma!"

Seeing me safe on the ledge, Ma smiled. Her hair had come undone and separated into wet seaweed strands down her shoulders. Her face was streaked with rain—or maybe tears. I would have expected her to look panicked or angry, but her face melted from a smile to a mix of surprise and resignation. "I can't make it," she said.

I crouched on hands and knees, still panting, staring down at the water, sensing its power and pull. For a moment—just a moment—I imagined sliding down to Ma. If we stopped fighting the current, it would be over in minutes. Our bodies would be dashed against the rocks; our lungs would fill with water. I might catch one last glance at Ma's battered body as it was tossed from boulder to boulder, and then—nothing. What kind of hubris had made us think we could cross a continent? Our pride would be the death of us.

No, it wouldn't. Not today. All I had to do was help Ma up to the ledge. I shouted over the roar of wind and water. "At least try!"

I watched Ma loop her satchel handles over her forearm and attempt the first foot- and handhold, but the bulk of the grips kept her from firmly bracing her arm against the side of the chute. She lost her tenuous hold and slipped back down.

"Let it go, Ma," I said. I motioned tossing her satchel into the river so she could climb unencumbered, but she shook her head. She lifted the bag toward me, indicating I should catch it.

I shook my head, but she nodded again. She was so gosh-awful stubborn. I'd just have to get her bag and hope to get her up here, too, before she was swept away. I lay down at the edge of the ledge, water streaming under my poncho and skirts, and stretched down my arms. She shifted her position several times, apparently feeling with her feet underwater for a place between rocks to wedge her feet while she got ready to throw.

She lifted her satchel two-handed behind her head for an overhand throw, still fighting for her balance in the river. The satchel sailed up toward me and my fingertips grazed one rain-slicked end, but it slipped away from me like a greased pig. Ma threw her hips forward to trap the bag between her body and the rocks and snatched a handle before it could be washed away in the river, still rising minute by minute.

She rested her forehead against the wall, her back heaving as she gulped in air. Then she clutched her bag for another try.

"Forget the bag, Ma!" I wasn't sure she could hear me, so I mimed again throwing the bag into the river. "Just get yourself up here."

She shook her head and flung the bag again. This time I hooked two fingers on the handle long enough to get a two-handed grip on it, and rose to my knees to shove it to the back of the ledge. Now for Ma.

She made a weak try at the first foothold and slipped down again into the water.

"You just have to make it the first few feet on your own, Ma. Once you're partway up, I can help you from here." I waved a loop of my satchel's rope handle over the edge. "See, Ma?" I began to fumble with the knots that connected the rope to my satchel, but rain had swollen the knots into place like glue. I sobbed with frustration. Then I remembered Arthur's penknife. "Hang on, Ma! I'll have a rope for you in a minute!" I sawed frantically at the rope with the little knife, but it was so dull that I despaired of slicing through in time to save Ma.

She made it up one handhold, two, three, while strand by strand the fibers on the rope snapped. Her fingertips were white with the cold and pressure of clutching at the merest knobs of rock. "Clara, I can't!" she wailed as one foot lost its purchase on the rock and she started to slide down the chute.

"Don't you dare leave me alone here!" I shouted, still sawing at the rope. I jerked once, again, and ripped the last few strands of rope from the short leather handle. "Here, Ma!" I leaned over the ledge and dangled the three feet of rope toward Ma as she started to slip another foot down the slide.

Her feet were just inches above the churning rapids. An uprooted twenty-five-foot pine, tossing like a twig in the river, hurtled toward Ma and threatened to sweep her off her slippery hold.

I cautiously edged another two inches forward. "Up, Ma!" I screeched. "Handhold six inches straight up with your left hand." Her left hand groped the rock like a blind crab and found the wedge of rock to cling to. Just as she shifted her weight to her higher handhold, the pine tree swept past, brushing Ma's skirts and dousing her with spray. Ma seemed oblivious to her near miss with death and continued her tortuous climb.

Right foot searching, finding. Left foot searching, finding. Right hand reaching, reaching. Fingertips finding the frayed end of the rope. I tried to look only at Ma and not the rapids below as I slithered another four inches toward the edge and locked my ankles around the base of a scrub pine behind me.

When Ma grasped the end of the rope, I felt the pull from my hands to my ankles. The intense pressure abated as Ma found a place for one foot and took most of her weight off the rope. "One more and you're up, Ma!"

Ma took two shuddering breaths and tightened her grip on the rope. "I'm pulling on three," I said. She nodded.

"One." Check ankle grip. "Two." Check grip on the knot. "Three!" I tried to flex my knees toward the tree as I pulled hand over hand on the rope to bring Ma closer to the ledge. My temples throbbed and my arms and knees shuddered with the tension as I finally reached Ma's hands and dragged her up beside me. Her knuckles were bloody and she'd ripped the front of her poncho as she slid up on the ledge, but we were together, above the water. Gasping and shaking, we pushed ourselves back on our seats as far as we could, wedged our satchels between our feet, and collapsed against the rock wall.

I leaned my head back and let the rain cool my flushed face. We were still alive. I tried to laugh. "This will be another chapter for your book, Ma." I wrapped an arm around her shoulders and leaned my head against hers to reassure myself that she was still here, with me, and not swept away. She nudged her head against mine in answer.

"You can write this chapter," she said.

CHAPTER 18

AFTER THE FLOOD

August 11, 1896–Day 98

The ledge of our salvation, Wyoming

I WOKE to swooping and chattering siskins and finches. Was there anything more beautiful than sunrise when you thought that you would die before another morning? My teeth ached from chattering all night. My shoulders and hands throbbed from clutching the tree. I was starving. But the sky was clear and we were still alive.

The only proof of yesterday's maelstrom was the charred stump of the tree struck by lightning and the flotsam of uprooted bushes left behind by the receding water, reduced by now to an innocent trickling stream. Compared to yesterday's ear-numbing thunder, roaring water, bruised muscles, terror, despair, hope, and relief, Mica Creek was just an imitation of real life. I felt like I had not been totally alive before this day.

If I did write the chapter about the storm, how would I begin? With the storm? With our argument before the storm? My teacher had convinced me that I wasn't a natural-born writer, but the only way to get better was to practice. I scooted back on the ledge, took out my journal, and began to write.

When Ma woke, she stood and saluted, as if we had just completed a successful mission. "You can't let fear of dying keep you from living the life you want," she said.

Was that bravado for my benefit, or hers?

"I intend to keep my guardian angel busy," she said.

As I put my writing away, I said, "Your angel must have a whole flock of apprentices to keep up with you, Ma."

Still perched on our ledge, we doctored each other's barked knuckles and I flexed my fingers until I regained enough dexterity to retie my rope to my satchel. A length of rope, given to us by a lonesome stationmaster. Had he any idea that it would save Ma's life three months later? I had already forgotten his name among the list of more than fifty people we had stayed with so far.

While I was fussing with my rope handle, Ma kneeled to fumble in her bag and unfold the oilskin she kept wrapped around her letter from Mayor Belt, *cartes de visite*, and copies of our picture. "These papers are why I needed you to save the bag," she said. "Thanks for saving me, too," she said with a smile that quickly faded as she turned serious. "If something did happen to me — if I couldn't go on for any reason — would you continue on your own?" She stressed the word *any*.

"But I promised Pa…" My voice quavered. I didn't want to think — not for an instant — of having to leave Ma behind someplace and going on.

Ma thrust her papers toward me. "Maybe you should carry these."

I kept my hands at my side. "If we can both survive flood and lightning, highwaymen, lava fields, and snowstorms in the Blues, we can both make it through anything. We'll be celebrating my birthday in New York."

Ma grasped one of my hands and gently raised it toward the papers in her other hand. She nudged the papers against my closed fist, like a cat wanting her chin scratched. When I opened my hand, Ma slipped the oilskin pouch into it. I was now the keeper of the papers. Did Ma think I had a better chance of surviving this trip, or was it her way of admitting that I was as important as she was to the success of this walk?

Ma finger-combed her hair and twisted it into a tidy knot. When she threw back her shoulders and raised her chin, she could have been the model for a statue glorifying indomitable American womanhood. "At least one of us has to make it to New York, so men can't say women are too frail for such a venture, or quit too easily. I have no patience for people who accept whatever life gives them without a fight," she said. "'God's will,' they say. Well, I say, 'With God, all things are possible.' The worst is behind us. Once we get to the plains, it's just a flat walk in the field to New York."

CHAPTER 19

WE GET LETTERS

August 16, 1896–Day 103

Laramie, Wyoming

L AST NIGHT we camped along the Laramie River with the Arapaho. Taking pity on us for our lack of survival skills, two of the women showed us how to roast sego lily bulbs and dry grasshoppers and crickets in the sun. Once the crickets and 'hoppers were ground fine as flour and mixed with seeds, I just held my breath and swallowed my share. Hunger is the best sauce, they say. I'd have to describe them to Johnny and Arthur in my next letter. This morning we traded pictures of ourselves for beaded hair ornaments, which I will save for Ida and Bertha.

Our canteens were empty, but I learned in the most stomach and gut-wrenching way not to drink alkali water. American womanhood was about to shrivel to empty husks and float away like thistledown.

Dry as I was, my curiosity was still healthy enough to investigate a glint of something shiny at the end of one of the railroad ties twenty or so feet ahead. I picked up two bottles of clear, pure water and stomped down on a bit of paper that had been under the bottles before it could blow off to Kansas.

"Water!" I croaked, waving the bottles like flags. Since our pastor at home used grape juice for communion, I had never tasted wine, but I was sure no wine or magic elixir could have tasted sweeter than that water. I closed my eyes to savor the taste, and carefully recapped the bottle.

While Ma drank, I picked up and read the paper I had trapped under my foot: "For the walking ladies." I looked around for chimney smoke or any other signs of a house, but there was nothing. We were in the middle of nowhere, and water had miraculously appeared. Ma would have claimed special delivery from one of her guardian angels, but I knew there had to be an earthly deliverer out there somewhere.

Twenty minutes later, we passed two gandy dancers pumping their cart along the track, with their mallets and burlap bag of supplies. I raised a bottle and shouted, "Was it you?" They did not stop, but waved shyly back. I blew them a kiss.

More bottles and canning jars of water appeared every five or ten miles for the next month. There must have been an organized campaign to keep us alive, with telegraphers sending word of our progress, letting railway workers and townspeople know when we were expected through. Sometimes the bottles were still cool, even when we saw no one. Other times we'd see a shy child or farm wife standing back from the track, shading her eyes with one hand and waving as we passed. We left our bottles at the next station we passed through, and assumed they somehow got back to their owners. I did not believe in Ma's guardian angels, but I had plenty of proof of the kindness of strangers.

I smiled as I read Ma's fourth report to Miss Waterson. For the first time it read from Helga *and Clara* Estby.

> To: *Miss A. J. Waterson, 95 William Street, New York City, New York*
>
> From: *Helga and Clara Estby*
>
> Monthly Report #4: *Greeley, Colorado*
>
> Miles covered, August 5–September 3: *335*
>
> Notes: *Survived flash flood.*

September 9, 1896 – Day 127

Denver, Colorado

The reporter would have been more interested in us if we had discovered another gold deposit, but perked up at Ma's account of my shooting a man in Oregon and our camp out with Indians. As we left the newspaper office, the reporter gave Ma a free copy of a pamphlet they'd printed on Colorado mining. Remembering how Ma had tried to send Pa to Colorado to find us a mine two years ago, I was sure she'd read that pamphlet from first word to last.

At the post office, she sat and read her pamphlet while I stood in line at the general delivery window. Would there be a letter from Salt Lake City? As the clerk left the counter to look for our mail, I watched the second hand on the wall clock make one circuit, two circuits, three. At last the clerk returned with a stack of letters, which I flipped through with trembling fingers. A letter from Pa, from Ida and Bertha, from Olaf, from Miss Waterson, and yes! Mr. Doré!

As I walked slowly back toward Ma's bench, I studied his envelope. A drop of brown liquid had smeared the word *Colorado* in the address. I smelled the envelope but couldn't tell if it was coffee or tea. I didn't know him well enough to guess. Had he written it at the office, or from home? I realized I didn't even know where *home* was for him. Did he have a room in a boarding house, or still live with his parents — or was he already married with a home of his own?

Still clutching his letter, I sat next to Ma on the bench while she opened the letter from Pa. She scanned the letter, gasped, and handed it to me.

The letter — in Norwegian, of course — covered only half a page.

Dear Helga,

Olaf has been sent to the sanatorium with the diphtheria.
We made it safely through harvest, but prices were not good.
I miss you, Mrs. Estby. I hope you and Clara are safe and can
come home soon.

> *Your husband,*
> *Ole*

> *P.S. I am too old to be looking for another wife, so take*
care of yourself.

> *Love, O.E.*

"I lost baby Ole, then Henry, and now I may lose Olaf!"

"But Olaf sent a letter, too, so he can't be dying." I shuffled through the stack and checked the postmark; Olaf had mailed his letter over a week after Pa's, and addressed it in a strong hand.

As Ma ripped open his letter, I said, "Diphtheria is more dangerous for little ones than young men." I put one arm around her shoulder. "He'll be fine soon. I know it." I lied. I didn't know it at all. Oh, why were we so far from home when our family needed us?

Ma's voice was hoarse at first, but grew clearer as she continued to read.

Sacred Heart Sanatorium

Dear Ma and Clara,

As I'm sure Pa and Ida have told you, I am recuperating from diphtheria in the sanatorium here in Spokane. The food is boring and the days are boring, too.

At least I waited to get sick until after the wheat was in. It threatened rain the week of harvest, so everyone worked clear through moonlight every night. I don't think anyone slept more than four hours a night for a week. After all that work we'll still have to borrow money for next year's seed again.

Clara, you will be amazed to hear I have read two books, cover to cover, this month!

> *Your loving son (and brother),*
> *Olaf*

Ma refolded the letters from Pa and Olaf and slipped them in her pocket. She was dry-eyed now, but her shoulders drooped. We were always a year behind, no matter how hard everyone worked.

I read Ida's letter aloud.

Dear Clara,

Olaf said he was so bored having to stay in bed in the sanatorium that he would write letters to everyone, and you know how he hates to write. I haven't been allowed to see him yet, but the receptionist let me drop off a plate of potato lefse and a jar of Pa's pickled herring. Tell Ma not to worry about Olaf. He's so tough it's hard to imagine anything short of a ton of bricks knocking him down for long.

Don't let Olaf tell you he was the only one who worked hard at harvest. Bertha and I just about died in the kitchen keeping everyone fed. I swear each man in the crew could eat a pan of biscuits and a whole plum pie by himself.

Tilda's wedding was beautiful! Everyone brought in

flowers from their gardens and we set them out in vases all across the front of the church. And her dress — her mother made it with white silk and Brussels lace appliqué.

I know Ma is worried about losing the farm, but Olaf will be carpentering in Spokane as soon as he gets out of Sacred Heart, and I know I could get a job as a shop girl in Spokane. I guess what I'm saying is, don't risk your neck on Ma's scheme to save the farm. With Pa, Olaf, and you and me all earning money in town, we could have a nice apartment. It wouldn't be the slums that Ma keeps threatening us with. I miss you. I'd rather have you and Ma home safely than all the money in New York.

Love, Ida

I passed the letter from Ida on to Ma to read, and while she was occupied with that, I read the letter from Salt Lake City.

August 20, 1896

Dear Miss Estby,

I couldn't help smiling as I pictured your mother curling hair for an entire band of Ute Indians. Our newspaper editor said it wasn't his policy to publish personal essays, but don't give up writing. With interest high in the vanishing old West, someone will want your pieces.

My news will hardly be as interesting as yours, but I will take your giving me your itinerary as leave to continue correspondence.

Most sincerely,
Charles Doré

P.S. One advantage of a black bicycle is that it is easy to find matching paint to fill in scratches. C.D.

P.P.S. If your mother had accepted the three Indian horses in trade for you, you would certainly have something more to write about, but I confess I am relieved that she decided she valued your company more than the three horses. Besides, you are worth at least four horses. C.D.

Not even the Salt Lake City newspaper wanted my story! Mr. Doré was probably just saving my feelings to say the paper didn't publish personal essays. Oh, *uff da.*

Disappointment constricted my chest, hurt my throat, and gave me a headache behind the eyes. The writing on the letter blurred as I tried one last time to find some good news in it. He did say I was worth at least four horses.

I looked up as Ma finished the letter from Miss Waterson. Judging from her expression as she handed it to me to read, Miss Waterson had not written with good news, either.

Dear Mrs. Estby,

Our contract allowed extensions of time for unpreventable delays such as illness. Getting lost is not an unpreventable delay but simple carelessness. Your walk is supposed to be a demonstration of women's intelligence and resourcefulness; so in the future, pack sufficient water and learn to use a compass properly.

I am not entirely unsympathetic, however. Although I will not grant an extension of time for the three days you were lost,

I will allow two days' extension for the time you were recovering from sunstroke.

> *Sincerely,*
> *Miss A. J. Waterson*

CHAPTER 20

THERE'S GOLD IN THOSE HILLS

September 10, 1896–Day 128

Denver, Colorado

SOMETIME between midnight and dawn, Ma nudged my shoulder and whispered, "Get up, Clara. We need to get an early start to Cripple Creek."

"*Uff da,*" I moaned. The bed creaked as I rolled over and snuggled more deeply into the covers. Then what Ma had said hit me and I bolted upright and forced my eyes open. "Cripple Creek?" I croaked. "That's the wrong direction."

"Remember when I wanted Pa to go to Cripple Creek? He wouldn't go, but this is our second chance."

By the light of the bedside candle, Ma read from the

pamphlet the numbskull at the newspaper office had given her on Colorado mining.

"Luck is with us; don't you feel it?" Ma said.

"What I feel is that for over four months we've nearly killed ourselves walking toward New York and it will all be for nothing if we miss our deadline so you can see some cockamamie gold mine."

"Humph!" Ma continued to flip pages in her booklet.

"Ma, that brochure is just hoopla and snake oil. The stores selling pickaxes made more money than ninety-nine percent of the miners." I grabbed the pamphlet. Ma tugged back. The pages ripped.

"Now see what you've done!" Ma held her ragged half of the pamphlet toward me reproachfully.

"I don't want to hear any more about those mines. We didn't get an extension for the days we were lost in Idaho, so we're twelve days behind now — we can't waste time on a detour. The bet is a sure thing if we just keep going. This gold nonsense?" I threw my pages of the pamphlet in the air.

Ma dived to pick them up and began to piece pages together on top of the bed.

I heaved my seat down on the bed. "Ma, look at me — look — *are* we trying to win or not?"

Ma pressed her lips into a sharp line and did not take her eyes from the pieces of the pamphlet as her fingers fluttered to reassemble them. Once she satisfied herself that all pieces were in place, she looked up.

I unfolded the map from her satchel and pointed out Denver and Cripple Creek. "Round trip it's at least one hundred and fifty miles, hiking at altitudes of up to ninety-five hundred feet. We'd squander another week—maybe two—getting there and back on course again. And what are you planning to do when we get there? We don't have a claim, and if we start digging on someone else's claim we're likely to get shot."

"Don't be so melodramatic, Clara. We can go to Cripple Creek and still get to New York on time." She leaned over the map and tapped a finger on the yellow rectangle of Nebraska and the orange of Iowa. "It's so flat, we can make up time there," she said.

"You started out to walk across the country and now you want to play gold miner. I think that's why Pa said he'd only let you go if I came with you—not only to keep you safe, but to keep you from flying off-course with some harebrained idea."

Ma scowled.

I continued my argument. "Why did we even leave home if you don't mean to win? With ten thousand dollars we could pay all our debts, all of us children could go to college, or you could set up Ida in her own hat shop and buy farms for all the boys. You said you were on this walk for the sake of the family, but I have to wonder if that's true. Maybe you're the one who wanted a change from Mica Creek and made up this walk as an excuse to get away."

When Ma stopped fluttering and went statue-still, I dared to hope I was getting through to her. "You were the one who said we can't afford to lose the farm. 'Without the land we starve' is what you said."

Ma sat, refusing to look at me. I took out Pa's owl and held it inches from her face. "Think of Pa. Think of Olaf, Ida, Bertha, Johnny, Arthur, William, and Lilly. They're all at home rooting for you, Ma."

At home, between the times she fought the dismals or the whirlwinds, we enjoyed blessed normal periods. Ma stretched a few pennies' worth of thread into a lace collar for Lilly to rival anything the Astors or Vanderbilts wore. She made prizewinning jams, she coached Arthur with his spelling, cut down one of her own dresses for Ida to wear for a dance. At the end of the day, she rocked Billy and Lilly on her lap and sang them her silly off-key lullabies. At these times, she was the best mother in Mica Creek. I wanted that version of my mother back.

I sagged when Ma stood, slipped on her shirtwaist, and fastened her skirt instead of coming back to bed. Circles of pink bloomed on her cheeks, and her eyes caught sparks from the flickering candle. I knew the pattern, and dreaded what might come next. A week from now she could burn herself out and she would be in bed again, more than a thousand miles from home, and more than a thousand miles from New York.

With fumbling fingers I refolded the map and stood as Ma laced up her shoes and started toward the stairs.

It would have been easier to persuade iron shavings to ignore the pull of a magnet than to persuade Ma to ignore the pull of gold. I stood at the top of the stairs, a hand over my mouth, blinking back tears. When Ma was like this, it was impossible to reason with her.

I had started the walk believing we might only be gone for a month or two before Ma ran out of steam and we returned home. Now—even though we were nearly two weeks behind schedule—I had almost dared to dream that we might reach New York and come home with enough money to fund a better future for everyone in the family. But not if we lost another two weeks on this crazy detour to Cripple Creek. I was almost mad enough to set off to New York by myself and try to collect from Miss Waterson, but not mad enough to forget my promise to Pa.

In five seconds I was scrambling into my clothes, sliding on dirty stockings, and skipping half the eyelets as I laced my boots. I blew out the candle and clomped down the stairs after Ma.

Mrs. Dawson, our hostess for the night, was standing at the door, watching Ma stride out on her new course toward Cripple Creek. She turned to me as I took the last two stairs in a leap. "You don't have to be off before breakfast, do you? I have the sourdough starter going for my specialty..."

My stomach rumbled at the thought of sourdough pancakes, but I looked anxiously at Ma's retreating back. I hesitated at the door just long enough for an apology. "Sorry to run, but when Ma gets it in her head to go, there's no stopping her." I ran after Ma, satchel banging against my thigh.

September 14, 1896—Day 132
Near Pike's Peak, Colorado

We only walked eighteen miles yesterday, and we were falling farther behind every day. At this altitude, we had to stop and rest every mile or so. We hardly spoke to each other, mile after mile, hour after hour.

We followed the Midland Terminal tracks around Pike's Peak and then to Gillett. We looped around the bottom half of Cow Mountain; looped northwest, south, and up and down Grassy Gulch; past Bull Cliff, Battle Mountain, Big Bull Mountain; and in to Victor.

It would have been another three miles from Victor to Cripple Creek as the crow flew, but since locomotives couldn't handle steep grades and we were following the tracks, we had to wind through the low spots between mountains. We slogged on and endlessly on, around Squaw Mountain, Elkton, Anaconda, Gold Hill, and Signal Hill. As we passed through wooden snow sheds that protected tracks at the bases of steep hills, we met men stationed inside to put out any fires the engines might spark. At each station, I fell to my knees and drank like a thirsty mule directly from their buckets.

I was scared to think of trying to take care of Ma so far from home. My nose was so dry that it bled, and I didn't even have the breath to scream at the frustration of wasting time zigzagging southwest through the mountains instead of getting

closer to New York. Every few steps I took out my frustration
on a rock and kicked it, pausing to watch it tumble over the side
of the narrow ledge the tracks ran on, and down hundreds of
feet into the ravine below. Our hopes of making it to New York
were tumbling along with the rocks.

Gasping for breath, I dropped my bag and collapsed on it,
but I didn't get a chance to rest. My bag upset the delicate balance
of the ragged slide of rocks on the uphill side of the track, and
rocks bigger than my head began to clatter down. In my panic to
avoid being swept over the brink in a roaring rockslide, I leaped to
the side and nearly lost my balance in the gravel. While I was still
tottering, I was startled anew with a rattle that sounded like the
frenetic buzz of a hundred riled-up bees. Something living took
shape in the waves of heat radiating from the mountainside.

It was strange the things you noticed when you thought you
were going to die. Close up, the scales on a rattlesnake looked
like the scales on a pine cone, though a pine cone didn't breathe,
rattle, and raise its head.

The snake opened its mouth and darted its forked, licorice-
black tongue up and down to taste the air for me. I turned,
stumbled, and screamed when a sharp pain slashed through my
ankle. As the snake slithered out of sight back into the rock
pile, I was sure I felt its venom working through my leg, swelling my body inch by inch with poison.

I can't remember how we got to Cripple Creek. I awoke alone
in a strange room, stretched out on a tufted divan in someone's

parlor. From the adjacent room, pottery and metal clinked and aromas of fried beef and onions drifted in.

Cutting through a mild hubbub of men's voices was a woman's voice...a familiar voice. "Ma?"

Her voice halted in midsentence. Rapid footsteps approached my room. "You're awake!" Ma covered the space between the door and the divan in three vigorous strides. "How's your snakebite?" she said cheerfully.

At my shocked expression, she said, "Just kidding. All the way here you were mumbling about a rattlesnake bite, but at that altitude he probably didn't have the energy to bite. You just sprained that ankle jumping out of the way."

"Hurts though," I said. "Let me look." I boosted myself upright against the sloped side of the divan.

Ma hiked my skirt up to my knee and unwrapped the dishtowel that had been holding chunks of ice in place. My ankle was puffed up to twice its normal size, and looked like I'd rubbed blackberry juice on it. I winced.

"It'll look worse before it looks better," Ma said as she rewrapped my ankle. "At least I found us a nice place for you to recuperate. Mrs. Fitzwilliam—this is her house and restaurant—said we can stay as long as I keep bringing in customers to hear about our adventures." Ma kneeled and stroked my hair back from my forehead. "Would you like something to eat?"

At my weak nod, she returned with a tray of soup, slabs of bread slathered in butter, and a cup of coffee. "You know I don't approve of coffee for young folks, but I guess you could use some perking up."

Ma offering me coffee? It was as good as an apology for dragging me off-course into the mountains. Despite Ma spoiling me something awful over the next few days, I wrote a self-pitying letter to Charles.

I made more of my ankle than I needed to when I saw its effect on Ma. She always claimed she didn't have control over her ups and downs, but in a heroic effort to help me, she broke free of her gold fever, as if waking from a spell. It also helped that the miners she entertained with her stories confirmed my earlier guess that most of the good claims were already taken.

The next morning, as she held another ice bag on my ankle, she said, "If I try something like this detour again, you have my permission to put me in a harness and drag me to New York City."

I smiled halfheartedly. When Ma promised no more detours, I knew she meant it; but if another fancy took hold of her brain, who knew if she would be able to resist it?

On the third day, Ma spread her maps on my lap as I lay propped up on the bed, another ice bag on my ankle. "We have a thousand miles of flat ground until we get to Pennsylvania," Ma said. "And since the eastern half of the country is more settled, we should find someone willing to take us in every night. If we start each day rested and fed, we should make thirty miles a day."

I was not as sanguine in my estimates as Ma, but we could still make New York in time if we got an extension. By the tracks it was about eighteen hundred miles between Denver and New York City. At just twenty miles a day—though no days for rest or work—we'd need ninety days to get to New York. Ma wrote Miss Waterson asking for more time.

September 15

To: Miss A. J. Waterson, 95 William Street,
   New York City, New York

From: Helga and Clara Estby

My daughter sprained her ankle crossing the Rocky Mountains, so we are laying up in Cripple Creek. I request a two weeks' extension of our deadline to allow time for her ankle to heal.

My ankle still throbbed at night, but it wasn't as bad as I had made it out at first. Although Ma asked for a two-week extension, with the aid of a donated crutch I was on the road again in five days.

CHAPTER 21

NEBRASKA LETTERS

Letters sent, October 5–October 11, 1896

To: Miss A. J. Waterson, 95 William Street,
  New York City, New York

From: Helga and Clara Estby

Monthly Report # 5: Kearney, Nebraska

Miles covered, September 5–October 5: 443

Notes: Clara is mending; we are making good time again. We will attempt to see Mrs. William Jennings Bryan when we reach Lincoln.

Sunday, October 11, 1896
Lincoln, Nebraska

Dear Mr. Doré,

I apologize for burdening you with such a maudlin letter last time and vow to henceforth be a more cheerful correspondent. My first good news is that I no longer need my crutch and my ankle is healing, though slowly. My second good news is that Ma did not find gold in Cripple Creek. If she had found a nugget the size of a pinhead, she would still be playing prospector. At least she has rededicated herself to our walk and we are making up a little of the time we lost. I'm exhausted and often bored — so many miles of flat fields and scrub — but as Ma says, the worst should be behind us. Some days the only thing that keeps me going is the thought of winning the money so we can buy two train tickets home.

For my brothers' sakes, I had hoped we would get to see Buffalo Bill and Annie Oakley while we were in Nebraska, since the Wild West show train is crisscrossing the state this month, but instead we met the wife of someone nearly as famous!

We knew from the newspapers that Mr. William Jennings Bryan (Ma's choice for the next president) was campaigning in the Midwest, but she hoped to find Mrs. Bryan at home. Their house was ordinary. It had a friendly wraparound porch and a bicycle leaned up against a tree in the front yard. Mrs. Bryan herself opened the door, wearing a half-apron over her dress as if she had been doing some of her own housework.

You know how forward Ma is. She thrust out her hand, bold as a Bible salesman, and said we'd walked two thousand miles from Spokane, Washington, just to shake her hand and get her autograph.

Well, what could she do after that but invite us in?

I had scrubbed my hands at the railroad station before our visit, but when I looked at my rough, brown fingers around her dainty flowered teacup, I felt like I would never be clean enough for anyone's parlor again.

Mrs. Bryan asked politely about our walk, and Ma

explained the other reasons — besides meeting her — for leaving Mica Creek. When Mrs. Bryan's four-year-old daughter, Gracie, came in to claim her mother's lap, Mrs. Bryan lamented that no matter where she was, she felt duty calling her someplace else. If she was home with her children, she felt she should be helping her husband campaign; and if she was campaigning with her husband, she felt she should be home with her children.

Ma said she understood.

We even got to see the library where Mrs. Bryan works with her husband. (She is a lawyer, too!) I still thought her husband was longer on fiery speechmaking than statesmanship, but at least by marrying a woman like Mrs. Bryan he showed he believed women could use their brains without losing their hearts.

I didn't tell Ma, but after meeting Mrs. Bryan I was almost tempted to vote for Mr. Bryan myself. If I could vote.

> *Most sincerely,*
> *Miss Clara Estby*

P.S. I never asked you: Are you in favor of votes for women?

Letters received October 13, 1896, in Omaha, Nebraska

From: A. J. Waterson, 95 William Street,
New York City, New York

To: Helga Estby

Your request for a two-week extension of time is granted, but do not use your daughter's sprained ankle as an excuse to steal rides on the train. My spies are watching you to make sure you walk all the way.

Salt Lake City
September 25, 1896

Dear Miss Estby,

With your wager at stake, no wonder you were frustrated by your mother's detour to Cripple Creek. I have heard rumors of another gold find in the Yukon Territory, so perhaps your mother's next plan for making the family's fortune will be to send you to the Klondike!

As I predicted, I have no news to rival yours. I trust my best wishes for your ankle's complete recovery will be sufficient excuse for writing.

Truly yours,
Charles Doré

P.S. A friend of mine, Miss Ernestine Fleming, has asked me to ask you if you would visit the class of high school freshmen she teaches when you pass through Salt Lake City on your way back home. I would consider it a boon if you would, for it would boost me greatly in her esteem. C.D.

I nearly crumpled this letter and heaved it as far as it would sail, but I perversely read the postscript again. Miss Ernestine Fleming. Oh, *ish da!* I jammed the letter into my pocket. But why should I care if he was courting Miss Ernestine? I'd only met him twice and exchanged a few letters…but the way he looked at me…I thought for sure he was a kindred spirit.

I took the letter out of my pocket and read it yet again. He showed great tact in mentioning Miss Ernestine in an offhand way that let me know his heart was elsewhere without presuming that I had been thinking of him as more than a friend.

I wished I could think of a diplomatic way to tell Erick I thought of him as a friend, not a husband. I had already torn up three letters I had drafted in my journal. To be honest, though, it wasn't just wanting to be tactful that made me tear up those letters. I was also afraid to burn my bridges. Erick might be the only young man in the world who wanted a shy, gawky, gap-toothed girl for a wife. Did I want to spend the rest of my life alone?

At the sound of my sighs and paper rustling, Ma looked up from rereading her letters. Her eyebrows were raised, inviting me to share, but it was my life, and a decision I had to make for myself.

Miss Ernestine. Maybe lightning would strike her down as she hung the laundry, or her weak heart would fail at the shock of finding a pit in her plum pudding.

CHAPTER 22

THE SUFFRAGISTS

October 16, 1896—Day 164

Des Moines, Iowa

T THE office of the *Des Moines Register*, Ma launched into her standard talk as soon as she found a reporter to listen.

Then the reporter turned to me. I cringed as I waited for his question.

"Who do you think the young women of Washington State would vote for next month if they could?" he said.

It was the first time a man had asked me, Clara, what I thought about the presidential election. I shrugged. "I don't know what all the young women in the state think."

"Then what do you think?"

I looked at my hands, folded schoolgirl fashion on my lap. Right or wrong, I blamed our current Democratic president,

Calvin Coolidge, for the depression. William Jennings Bryan was another Democrat, so wouldn't the country be better off trying McKinley's ideas instead? But after meeting Mrs. Bryan, I wasn't so sure. Maybe I would vote for Bryan if I had the chance.

Just as I raised my head to speak, Ma jumped in with her opinion. "I would vote for William Jennings Bryan. Even the experts disagree about whether Bryan's free silver or McKinley's tariffs would pull us out of the depression. But Bryan is on the right side of the most important issue."

She pointed her finger at the reporter like a gun. "The most important issue in this election is simple: Does the female half of the population have the right to vote? Ex-slaves can vote, as long as they're male. Someone who can hardly read can vote, as long as he's male. It seems like criminals, idiots, and women are the only ones who can't vote." She put one hand on her hip, daring him to disagree with her.

He let off a belly laugh. "No fisticuffs, ma'am. You're among friends and preaching to the choir. The Iowa Equal Suffrage Association is meeting today to get ready for a demonstration on Election Day. You really should go."

"How far is it?" I probably sounded like a peckish child, but I didn't care. My ankle had started throbbing again, and the thought of having to make small talk with a roomful of women I didn't know gave me a stomachache. Before I could express dissent, the reporter whisked us off in a borrowed buggy to a meeting of the Suffrage Association.

Ma strode up the broad stone steps of a grand house and straight to the front door. I limped two steps behind. I wouldn't want to be here even if my shirtwaist were clean and pressed and I'd had a bath this week. Ma leaned over and flicked a few weeds and briars off my skirt and tucked straggles of hair behind my ears. "*Ja, da.* We'll pass."

As the door opened, we heard a babble of a lively discussion. The front hall was overdecorated with both lace undercurtains and velvet drapes. Oriental rugs covered almost every square inch of marble floor. The hall table was heaped with calling cards. Ma looked happy to have one of her own to hand to the maid. "The reporter in town told us about the meeting today," Ma said.

The maid opened a set of double doors and preceded us into the dining room. The babble of voices stopped as twenty-seven faces looked between the maid and our sorry selves. Despite being the daughter of Mica Creek's most notorious (well, only) suffragist, this was my first suffrage meeting.

The maid gave our card to the woman at the head of the table, who looked like someone's favorite schoolteacher, with round spectacles, curly graying hair, and tiny, plump hands. She read Ma's card aloud: "'Mrs. H. Estby and daughter, Pedestrians, Spokane to New York.' We've been reading about you!" she said. "I didn't remember your names, but I do remember the reporter's doubt that two women alone could set out across the country and reach New York alive." She grinned. "I'm happy to see you're proving them wrong."

"Ladies," she said, turning back to the table. "We are privileged to have with us two women who are risking their lives not only to save their farm, but in the cause of women's suffrage. These two women set off on a bold plan to walk clear across the country to New York with only what they carry in their satchels, without so much as a quilt or a frying pan." She went on for another five minutes, outdoing Ma in her talent for filling the air with words.

Each time she paused in her monologue praising our courage and the importance of our demonstration of woman's endurance and self-reliance, Ma opened her mouth to speak, but Mrs. Blackstone — for that was her name, as I learned — took a quick breath and beat her to the next word. Finally she wound down. "Mrs. Estby should be an inspiration to us all, as I'm sure she is to her daughter. We'll look forward to hearing from them after our business meeting, which I hope you will help me keep as brief as possible."

The room burst into applause, probably for the relief at hearing it would be a brief business meeting. Ma took the applause as approbation for her venture and nodded toward each cluster of ladies as graciously as a queen acknowledging her subjects. Ma immediately took a seat near the end of the table. I was left standing like the loser in a game of musical chairs. The committee reports droned on, but I was more interested in food arrayed on the buffet table at the side of the room. Once I'd had my fill of macaroons and tea breads, I scanned the women seated around the table, pencils in hand or holding a cup of tea. The overhead lamp glinted off a few diamonds or gold bands on ring fingers, but several left hands were bare. Not a one of those unmarried looked as if she lived in a gutter. They were proof that a woman had more choices than marriage or poverty.

Suddenly, everyone stood and shuffled to form a circle. Ma took my right hand, and a woman in a perfect pompadour and starched white shirtwaist took my left.

Mrs. Blackstone led off like a pastor with the responsive reading:

> If your husband asks you what you're serving for
> dinner, *(Mrs. Blackstone)*
>> *Tell him you want the vote. (All)*
> If he says he needs new shirt collars,
>> *Tell him you want the vote. (All)*
> If he asks you if you think it will rain today,
>> *Tell him you want the vote! (All)*

As the circle dissolved in grins and chatter, I struggled to stay close to Ma. But I quickly regretted it, because I was immediately swarmed by the inquisitive women. Ma, of course, was in her glory and described our trek like a dime novel:

"Turned out into a rainstorm!"

"Walking fifty miles in a single day!"

"Traversing the Blue Mountains in a ferocious blizzard!"

"Fighting off an evil assailant!"

Listeners rewarded Ma's storytelling with cries of astonishment, sympathy, and outrage.

"I can't believe any woman would let you be turned away into a rainy night in the middle of nowhere," Mrs. Blackstone said. "At least you have a place to stay tonight—right here with me."

I didn't even have time to finish my sigh of gratitude for a dry bed when the room erupted in helpfulness.

"Where are you planning to spend the night tomorrow?"

"Are you going through Indiana? I have an aunt in Fort Wayne."

"My sister's married to the stationmaster in Pittsburgh."

By the end of the evening I had the names and addresses of twenty-three women between Des Moines and New York City who would take us in or give us work. And those twenty-three women would know more people, who would know more people. Those names would be more precious than our maps and canteens.

CHAPTER 23

CHICAGO

November 4, 1896–Day 183

To: *Miss A. J. Waterson, 95 William Street,*
New York City, New York

From: *Helga and Clara Estby*

Monthly Report # 6: approaching Chicago, Illinois

Miles covered, October 5–November 4: 650

Notes: Have made good time on flat ground.

November 5, 1896 – Day 184
Hodgkins, Illinois
ELECTION DAY!

Ma fretted that we were only as far as Hodgkins, Illinois, on Election Day. She was sure she was missing a magnificent women's rally two days ahead in Chicago. I fretted that we had forty-one days to our revised deadline of December 16, and the rest of Illinois and all of Indiana, Ohio, Pennsylvania, and New Jersey to cross. We had no time for rallies.

She wrote ahead to the Marshall Fields store in Chicago to see if they would hire us to attract customers to their store with a talk about our travels. I still didn't like parading in front of strangers, but we could earn more money in an afternoon by modeling than we could in a week of scrubbing floors or laundry, and we had to get warmer clothes.

November 6, 1896–Day 185
Approaching Chicago

McKinley won! If we had already been in New York, we could have seen the election results cast up by a magic lantern against Pulitzer's New York World Building. Every time someone asked us if we had heard the news, Ma winced. At least we could both celebrate passage of the referendum giving Idaho women the vote.

As we walked along the tracks past frozen fields and orchards toward Chicago, we saw more and more itinerant men that the depression had left without work. Some greeted us as one of their own, calling out "Ho!" for fellow hobo as they passed by. I "ho'ed" back, for Ma and I were little better than beggar-tramps ourselves.

We washed in the train station and found our way to the offices of the *Chicago Post*. From there, we went to Marshall Field and Company's new store at State and Washington. Ida would be giddy at the thought of nine floors filled with beautiful goods from all over the world. I was too tired to be excited about acres of silk scarves and silver. I just wanted to earn enough money for a warm coat and hat.

The next day while Ma talked, I scanned the crowd, imagining that somewhere in the crowd Mr. Doré was poised with notebook and pencil. Ma slipped in a few references to women's votes as well as the superior qualities of the bicycle costumes we wore. After she told our sad story of Henry's death and debts that threatened our farm, she sold all but a few of her remaining pictures of ourselves. We made enough money for a hotel room tonight and wool coats, jaunty Tyrolean hats, and gloves.

November 9, 1896 – Day 188

Chicago, Illinois

This morning we collected mail before setting off for Indiana.

Dear Clara,

I hope you are getting adventuring out of your system and will be ready to settle down when you return. This winter I have started to make us a table and bed. Alma says she'd be so happy to

have another woman in the house she'd be willing to give up her
room and sleep in the kitchen until we get our own place built.
Could anyone ask for a nicer sister?

Oh, Clara, do not forget all those who wait impatiently
for your return.

Very truly yours,
Erick Iverson

"Oh, no!" I moaned.

Ma looked up from her letter from Pa.

"Erick is already making our wedding bed, and he's probably alerted the pastor to start announcing the wedding banns
three weeks before we are expected home so the wedding can
take place before I've even unpacked."

"I thought you were writing him a letter," Ma said.

"I tried, but I tore them up. I don't want to hurt his
feelings."

"Sometimes the kindest, gentlest way of saying no is
'no,'" Ma said. "Anything less than a firm refusal will let him
think he still has hope." Ma's face fell into a sad and wistful
expression.

At first I thought she was sorry for me, and then I wondered
—was it possible that that was how she ended up with Pa? That
he proposed, and although he was not a kindred spirit, he was so
kind and earnest that she couldn't find a way to refuse him?

I'd sit down and write that letter now. No—I'd write two

letters; one to Erick, and one to Ida to make sure the message
came across.

Dear Erick,

*Before we left, you honored me with your proposal. After six
months' consideration, I have concluded that the best answer for
both of our sakes is no. I'm sorry to have to convey this personal
decision by letter, but did not think it kind to make you wait
until my mother and I returned for my answer.*

I wish you all the best; you deserve it.

> *Sincerely,*
> *Clara*

Dear Ida,

*I have just written Erick with my refusal of his proposal. I do
not flatter myself to think he will mourn for me for long, but it
would ease my conscience if you could cheer him up if it looks
like he needs it.*

> *Your fond sister,*
> *Clara*

In my resolve to write to Erick, I had almost forgotten the letter
I had from Mr. Doré.

Salt Lake City

Dear Miss Estby,

*Thank you for your letter describing your meeting with Mrs.
Bryan. I used your description of the Bryans' house and quota-*

tions from Mrs. Bryan for an article in the Deseret Evening News (crediting you as my source), and relayed to our readers your news that you had safely crossed Nebraska. Perhaps you could become a freelance reporter, although I should warn you not many people are able to support themselves that way.

Miss Fleming claims she should be quite jealous of you, since I have gone to some effort to do something on your behalf, which I hope will have a salutary outcome. I have assured her that I am only doing it to ensure your willingness to speak to her class. You will, won't you?

Very truly yours,
Charles Doré

P.S. Be prepared for a possible surprise in your mail in Pittsburgh or New York.

CHAPTER 24

OHIO: WE MEET THE NEXT PRESIDENT

Thursday, November 26–Day 205

Big Prairie, Ohio

ODAY was my eighteenth birthday. Ma made no mention of it, so I didn't, either.

December 1, 1896

Dear Bertha and Ida,

When I get home, you can shake the hand that shook the hand of the next president of the United States! Canton was still celebrating when we arrived last Sunday. Red, white, and blue buntings draped from the buildings all along Tuscarawas Street. It looked like the Fourth of July except for the snow on the ground. Campaigning from home may have saved Mrs. McKinley's health, but it took a toll on their house. The porch steps had valleys worn in them from the thousands of people a day tromping up to see McKinley during his campaign.

I didn't know if the McKinleys would still be home to visitors, but I tried the line Ma had used with Mrs. Bryan: "My mother and I have walked three thousand miles from Spokane, Washington, to shake the next president's hand." The butler let us in.

As we entered, McKinley stood and crossed the room to us. Ma and I each gave a hint of a curtsey as we shook his hand. Mrs. McKinley sat crocheting in a small, elaborately carved rocker to the right of the parlor's bay window. She nodded toward two small damask chairs behind us.

It was so dim in the room that I wondered why Mrs. McKinley didn't light the double-globe gas lamp on the table beside her, but she explained that the light aggravated her headache. Besides, she didn't need any light to crochet by. She had crocheted so many slippers since phlebitis confined her to a chair that she could crochet them with her eyes shut.

You've seen his pictures in the newspaper: thin hair, bushy eyebrows, cleft chin, smooth-shaven. The only surprises were that he was little taller than I am (though larger in girth) and he looked younger than his pictures. He wore a frock coat, striped trousers, white pique waistcoat, gold watch, wing collar, and black silk tie, which Mrs. McKinley had made for him.

During our replies he often looked over at his wife, to see her response to us and affirm that she was not discommoded by our visit. His regard was so tender, so solicitous in every respect, I could see that reports of his devotion to her were not exaggerated.

Mrs. McKinley had cropped her wavy auburn hair to nape length and wore it parted severely in the middle and tucked behind her ears. She said she had cut her hair to reduce headaches from the weight of it, but I would be tempted to cut my own hair to make it easier to wash. Her dress was pale blue silk, and she wore a small diamond brooch at her throat. The rose-patterned wallpaper was similar to the paper in our bedroom at home.

Ma told Major McKinley he could make his place in history by supporting a constitutional amendment giving the vote to women, and I got out the Mayor Belt letter she'd been collecting signatures on so she could add McKinley's autograph.

As you may have guessed, the enclosed crocheted slippers are from the hand of the next first lady. Ma and I could not imagine putting our rough feet into such dainty, be-ribboned creations, so we are sending the slippers home so you two can be "ladies" instead.

I miss you both, and hope to see you all by Christmas.

Love, Clara

Dear Mr. Doré,

You may report that after crossing all of Indiana and over half of Ohio in two weeks, the two women walkers met President-Elect McKinley and his wife at their home in Canton, Ohio, on November 29. I am sorry to disappoint you in your prediction that I could become a freelance reporter. When I came into the presence of the next president of the United States, the details of my readings on tariffs fled my mind and I asked but the most simple-minded questions. In fact, we talked more about our trip *than his plans for this country. I shall have to think of another occupation, for Nellie Bly has no competition in me.*

> *Sincerely,*
> *Miss Clara Estby*

> *P.S. Did your mysterious venture have its intended "salutary outcome"?*
> *P.P.S. You may tell Miss Ernestine Fleming that I will be happy to visit her class if we pass through Salt Lake City on our way home. C.E.*

Of course I had no doubt that I could convince Ma to take a route far north or south of Salt Lake City on the way home. There was no reason to waste a train trip home going over the same ground we had covered on foot.

To: Miss A. J. Waterson, 95 William Street,
New York City, New York

From: Helga and Clara Estby

Monthly report # 7: Ambridge, Pennsylvania

Miles covered, November 5–December 5: 492

Notes: We called on President-Elect McKinley at his home in Canton.

CHAPTER 25

A LATE BIRTHDAY

December 6, 1896–Day 215

Pittsburgh, Pennsylvania

MA WAS as worried about my brother Olaf as she was about making it to New York by December 16. She was sure he had died in the sanatorium without her. He never would have contracted diphtheria if she and I had been home to help with harvest and he hadn't worked so hard. She shouldn't have named him Olaf; that name was too close to baby Ole, and he had died young so Olaf was going to die young, too. It was my fault; why hadn't I talked her out of this trip? It wasn't her fault; if the railroads and the banks didn't take advantage of hard-working farmers, we would not be about to lose the farm. It was her fault; if she hadn't insisted Pa build a house right away with borrowed money, we would not have been in debt. It was Pa's fault; if he had not hurt his back he could have earned more money carpentering last winter and we could have paid a little something on the taxes and mortgage.

Since we shared a bed or pallet every night, when she didn't sleep, I didn't, either. She poked me awake at two a.m., three-thirty a.m., and five a.m. to repeat her litany of fears for Olaf's health and blame for our circumstances. For three nights I was patient, but my ankle still throbbed and I was desperate for sleep. The fourth time she nudged me awake last night I shoved her back. "Just stop it," I hissed.

Worry and lack of rest had put black circles under Ma's eyes, and her lower lip trembled. How could I be so unsympathetic? I brushed the back of my hand across her cheek. "I'm sorry, Ma, I'm sorry. I'm just so tired." We both had to stay strong just a few more days. Then, as winners or losers, we could both give in to exhaustion and go to bed for a month if we needed it. At least this trip would be over.

Ma stared at me glassy-eyed, slack-mouthed. I touched her shoulder gently. "I'm sure Olaf is fine, we'll win the bet, and you'll be on the front page of the *New York World*." She did not respond.

I helped settle her under the covers and she closed her eyes, but I don't think she slept. I didn't, either, for a while, but the next time I opened my eyes it was six-thirty. Ma was already dressed and sitting quietly on the foot of the bed, holding Pa's watch, staring at the hands as they counted out the hours and minutes to our deadline.

At the Pittsburgh post office, Ma sent home another batch of journal notes and we picked up three letters from home and a thick envelope from Salt Lake City. I wanted to open it immediately to see if there was news about Mr. Doré's secret project, but Ma tugged on my elbow. "Let's check in at the newspaper and read our letters later, in private," she said.

The reporter at the *Pittsburgh Gazette* must have noticed the circles under Ma's eyes, so after a brief interview, he excused himself for a telephone call and came back with good news. "It's all arranged," he said. "You can spend the night at one of the nicest hotels in town. I said you'd be willing to talk to some of the guests after you've had a chance to rest, but I'm sure they won't keep you long."

Ma nodded a weak assent. Thinking of a hot bath and a warm bed, I gathered energy for a grateful grin.

As we entered our hotel room, I dropped my bag, sank to the floor, and leaned against the mahogany dresser as I waited to hear what was in Ma's letters. She sat on the bed and opened Pa's letter first. As she read it, color dotted each cheek. A smile spread from her mouth to her eyes as she looked up. "Olaf is home."

I remembered to breathe. "I knew he'd be fine." I opened the letter from Ida and Bertha first, saving Mr. Doré's letter for last. I unlaced my boots and propped my feet up on my satchel as I read. Ida's P.S. was provoking, but she had not meant it to be: "Happy 18th Birthday, Clara! What did you do to celebrate?" My answer, had she been here to talk to, would have been "nothing."

Ma extracted news from her letter from the boys. They closed with the words, "We love you, Ma. Come home soon."

She held up the last page so I could see Billy's wobbly *B* at the bottom.

Olaf was alive and her children still loved her. That was all Ma needed to restore her spirits. She hooked the curling iron over the chimney of the gas lantern to heat and took off her shirtwaist before washing her face and arms in the basin under the mirror.

I carefully slit the envelope from Mr. Doré and pulled out the first sheet on which he had written "Happy 19th Birthday!" He had drawn a clumsy garland of daisies around the message. Nineteen? If he had found out when my birthday was, why didn't he get my age right?

The second enclosure was an oblong slip of blue paper. The first line was a blank with my name filled in with elegant copperplate handwriting. To: *Miss Clara Estby.* The second line had pinprick holes in the shape of the number five. It was a check from Chase National Bank. "Five dollars!" I yelped. I felt Ma's eyes on me as I read the attached letters. The first was typed on the engraved letterhead of Street and Smith, Publishers.

Dear Miss Estby:

We are pleased to inform you that we have accepted your story, "Our Wilderness Salon" for publication in the January 3, 1897, issue of the Log Cabin Library. *We encourage you to think of us when you have another piece to submit.*

Sincerely,
Francis Shubael Smith

Dear Miss Estby,

As you will see from the enclosures, my secret deed at last had the desired result. I submitted the article first to Beadle Press, which publishes those dime novels your brothers probably read, but they never answered. Luckily, I sent them a copy I had typed in duplicate, so I still had your original and the carbon, which I sent on to Street and Smith. Let this be a lesson: Don't give up too soon. I had eleven rejections on one of my stories before it was published.

When the editors asked for information about you, I realized I didn't know anything about you except that you were an adventurous, intelligent young woman of pleasing appearance who was born in Minnesota. With that lead, I thought I could at least find out for them how old you were, so I wired the Minnesota Vital Statistics Bureau. I not only found out that you were born in 1877, but that your first check as a writer might arrive in time for your birthday.

I trust that your journey has been smooth and swift, and my greetings reach Pittsburgh in time.

> *Sincerely,*
> *Charles Doré*

P.S. Congratulations! I remember what a thrill it was to have my first article published.

I stood and waved the check and Mr. Doré's letter like flags. "I'm published!" I held the check and letter against my heart. I was not just Helga and Ole Estby's daughter. I was Clara Estby, author, and esteemed correspondent of Mr. Charles Doré, of the Salt Lake City *Deseret Evening News.* I kissed his signature.

"Olaf is well, you've published a story, and we have a grand room tonight. This will be a day to remember," Ma said. "You might want to check a mirror before we go downstairs, though. You have a smudge of ink on your mouth."

I touched my lips with my fingertips and all but swooned as I thought of Charles's hand, which had held the pen that held the ink that was on my lips. Of course I only thought of Mr. Doré as a friend—I was just grateful to him for finding a publisher for me. I felt no ill will toward Miss Fleming. She was lucky to have Mr. Doré, but what was a beau compared to the thrill of a career?

I crawled up on the bed to show Ma the check and the letters. "The five dollars is for my article about the time we camped with the Ute Indians and you showed them how to use your curling iron."

"When did you send that in?"

"I didn't—at least not to the publisher. I sent it to Mr. Doré for his newspaper and he sent it on to Street and Smith."

Ma picked up the check. "You could use another pair of shoes," she said.

I was not thinking about my thin soles then. "Ma, that's not all. Mr. Doré found out when my birthday was. The Minnesota records department had my day right, but they made a mistake on the year I was born. Mr. Doré thinks I'm nineteen, not eighteen."

Tears filmed Ma's eyes as she stared at Charles's birthday greeting.

"Oh, Ma, I don't mind that you forgot my birthday. You walked me clear across the country to meet the next president of the United States. That was the best present you could have given me." I started to hug her, but she shrank back.

She covered her face with her hands. "Newspapermen and their facts."

CHAPTER 26

MA'S REVELATION

December 6, 1896–Day 215

Pittsburgh, Pennsylvania

I SHIFTED sideways so I could see Ma's face. "What facts?"

The mattress jiggled as I crawled opposite her and sat tailor fashion, ready to listen. "If it's something about me, don't I have a right to know?" The only thing Mr. Doré had found out, assuming he was right, was the year I was born, and why should that cause such distress?

Oh, *du er dum, du!* I blushed. Maybe—I caught my breath just to think it—Ma had had to marry Pa, and didn't want anyone in Mica Creek to know she'd had a hurry-up wedding.

"Ma," I said, "I think I understand. Pa must have had more sweet talk in him than anybody knew, to talk you into rushing things." I smiled a worldly, woman-to-woman smile.

"No, Clara, you don't understand at all." Ma looked down at her lap and swallowed. Then she lifted her head. "Ole is not your father. Your father — your natural father — is Patrick O'Keeffe."

"O'Keeffe! How can someone I've never heard of be my father?" My voice rose to a decidedly un-worldly-wise squeak as I unfolded my legs and slid off the bed.

Ma sighed. "You've lived on a farm; I shouldn't have to explain that."

"I don't mean that part…I mean…I guess…" The walls of the room started to shift back and forth, like the pendulum on a clock; even when I closed my eyes I felt like the room was rocking and I had to hang on to the bedpost to keep from falling.

Ma pulled away from the headboard and sat stiffly. "Patrick…Patrick was a young man back in Michigan. The man I loved before Ole."

The horrified look on my face prompted Ma to explain. She put one hand to her heart, as if covering a scarlet *A* beginning to sprout like Hester Prynne's on her shirtwaist. "He wasn't just any boy…We were going to get married when he finished college."

"So why didn't you get married?"

"We would have, if his mother hadn't come down with consumption. Her doctor suggested she move to the mountains to clear her lungs. His father was dead, so Patrick planned to help her through the summer and he'd see me again before he went back to college. In July, I realized I was pregnant."

Heat radiated from my chest to my cheeks. I clung tighter to the bedpost. "My mother pregnant and no husband. I laugh to think about all your Sunday school advice. 'Don't go out walking alone with Erick; don't let him kiss you until you're engaged...' Didn't your mother give you the same advice? The rules never seem to apply to you, do they? You do whatever you want and excuse yourself with the thought that your love, your need to save the farm, your motives, are so pure, your needs so much stronger than any ordinary mortal's that whatever you do is justified." By now my cheeks felt fiery, my chest heaved, and my throat was sore from taming a shout down to a hoarse whisper.

I tried to work up steam for another rant, but it was hard to keep up momentum when Ma just sat there, immobile and expressionless. "If Pa hadn't been willing to marry you, everyone would say I was a b—" I couldn't say the word, not out loud. "Say something!" I picked up a pillow from the bed and threw it across the room, where it bounced off the window.

"I wouldn't undo anything I've done in my life. Even Patrick, if it meant there wouldn't be a Clara." She smiled gently.

"Why should I listen to anything you say — ever again?"

Ma massaged her temples, then let her arms drop limply to her sides. "Clara, who is better qualified than a woman who has had to live with the consequences..."

I roiled up again. "So that's what I am? A consequence of your bad judgment?"

"Oh, Clara, no..." Her face softened as she slipped off the bed and took both my hands. I tried to jerk my hands from her, but she would not let go.

"Clara, I know this must be hard for you, but let me finish. You and my other children are the best part of my life. What I meant by consequences was that I haven't seen my own parents since they sent me away with Ole. And as you know, those years in the soddy were not what I had been raised to expect for my life."

My hands were still tense in Ma's, but I did not interrupt.

"I gave up any hope of marrying Patrick to make sure you had a name and a home. I made a mistake, but I did my best to make it right for you. You mope and dither about what you should do with your life. I wish to heaven I'd still had as many choices at nineteen as you do now. You have no children, no husband to tie you to one place. You can stand on your own feet and go anywhere you want to." She waited for me to say something, but I just stood there with my mouth pressed shut.

I wanted to know—and didn't want to know—the details of how I ended up Clara Estby instead of Clara O'Keeffe. "So you were pregnant. What did you do?"

Ma looked away. "I wrote to Patrick. I didn't have a real address for him, just general delivery for the town in Colorado he thought they'd be moving to, but maybe they settled someplace else. When a month went by without a reply, I finally got the courage to tell my mother. She promised she'd think of something, and she did. A month later my mother had me married off to Ole, who worked for my stepfather. Ole had admired me, but without a farm or a business of his own, he never would have presumed to ask for me until then, when I desperately needed a husband. This was his chance to rescue me, you see? He gave his word that he would treat you as his own child. And he has been a good father to you, hasn't he?"

I was numb. "You've lied to me all my life...about Pa, even how old I was."

"I wasn't sure you were mature enough to understand. And I was right, wasn't I? I shouldn't have told you."

"But then I wouldn't have wondered why I was so different from Ida and all the others."

"Everybody's different. Ida is a happy gadabout and Bertha is a quiet, musical one—who knows where that came from—and it isn't because they're not full sisters; they're just their own people. You don't need the excuse of a different father to be a different person."

"Maybe...Oh, I don't know."

"Sit down and I'll brush out your hair. That used to soothe you when you were little."

Ma's face relaxed in recollection as her eyes followed a path from my hair to my eyes, nose, mouth, chin. "Your rounded cheeks and chin are his; your eyes are dotted with several colors, like his. I always thought you had his hair, too."

"Brushing my hair isn't going to make me forget that I just

found out that Pa is not my pa, my father ran off to Colorado instead of marrying you, I didn't know how old I was, and my name should have been O'Keeffe — O'Keeffe? Is that Irish? I'm not even Norwegian. I don't know what's true and what's not anymore."

My eyes widened as my memory latched on what Ma had said a few minutes ago. "Colorado! You said Patrick went to Colorado. That's the real reason you wanted to spend more time there, isn't it? You thought if we tromped through those mountains and talked to enough people you'd run across someone who knew where he was."

Ma sighed. "I heard…" She stopped and cleared her throat. "I heard he did come back to Michigan for me. I imagined how Patrick must have felt; his mother just recently buried, then coming back and finding out his faithless bride-to-be had already married someone else and moved to Minnesota. I wrote a letter to explain… I couldn't bear to have him think I hadn't loved him… I tore it up." For a moment Ma's face went blank; then she shook her head as if to shake unhappy memories away.

"Interviewers are waiting, Clara," she said briskly. She reached toward me, but I jerked my shoulder away.

Hearing how Ma had suffered blunted my anger, but I still wasn't up to a room of strangers. "Just go. I need time to myself," I said.

Ma closed the door so carefully, it hardly made a sound.

* * *

I shuffled to the bathroom to scrub off travel grime and neaten my hair, but I stopped in midscrub when my eyes met the eyes in the mirror. I was nineteen years old. Nineteen, with the eyes, full cheeks, and hair of a father I never met. What else did I inherit from him? Everyone had always said I was like Pa. My head ached, as if all the bits of memory in my brain were breaking loose from their old moorings and rearranging themselves to fit the new version of my history.

Hairpin by hairpin, I loosed my hair. Mrs. McKinley said she got headaches from the weight of her hair. I tipped my head back until I was looking at the ceiling and my hair brushed my skirt at the back of my knees. It was heavy, my hair that was the color of Patrick O'Keeffe's. Whether it was his fault or not, he left Ma when she needed him. How could Ma and Pa bear to look at me, knowing how much I looked like him?

A leather sharpening strop hung by a hook on the wall, but the hotel had not provided a razor to go with it. I dashed to the bedroom. A drawer in the desk had a postcard of the hotel and a letter opener, but the blade was not sharp enough. I threw the letter opener back in the drawer and dumped out my satchel on the bed, scrabbling through the pencil stubs, a flattened toothbrush, the last of a tin of toothpowder, a sliver of soap, and a bottle of iodine until I found Arthur's penknife.

I'd seen Pa use a strop and I used it now on the penknife. I stared into the round mirror. My pupils were so large that my eyes looked almost black instead of speckled blue and green. How bold was I? Short, like Mrs. McKinley's? Chin length?

What a mugwumping ditherer—I couldn't even decide how short to cut my hair.

I pulled a tress taut toward my shoulder and started sawing until the first clump came off in my hand—more than three feet of it. Oh, glory! What had I done? Courage; no turning back. I kept at it, pulling hunks of hair around from the back, bringing them to the same point on my shoulder, and hacking away. Each cut pulled at my scalp as I worked at it with the knife. Tears blurred my image in the mirror. I'd never get my hair into a braid now. It had taken eighteen—no, nineteen—years to grow it and now I was chopping it off in minutes. I was as impetuous and foolish as Ma.

I was left standing in a puddle of hair. Getting rid of the hair on the floor was like getting rid of a dead body. I opened pages of the complimentary copy of the newspaper and wrapped the hair in batches and put it in the wastebasket, nearly filling it. I ran a small strand through my hands. Near the tips, it was still baby blond, but at the upper end where I had cut, the hair had reached the sparrow-brown color I supposed it would be until it turned gray. I had cut off my past, whatever that was. For old times' sake, I coiled this one last strand and carried it back to the pile of belongings on the bed, opened my battered compass, and snapped the lid shut on the last of my long hair.

My stomach growled. Ma was probably getting dinner downstairs and talking to whoever had shown up at this late hour to see her. I wanted food, but didn't want to hear Ma rant about my hair, so I pulled it into a lump at the back and anchored it any which way with a dozen hairpins, then covered the mess with the Tyrolean hat I'd earned in Chicago.

As I left the room I looked back toward the bed and Mr. Doré's letter and the check. Did he have any idea what he had started with that inquiry to the Vital Statistics Bureau?

I followed voices through the lobby, the dining room, and through swinging doors into the kitchen, where a dozen or so hotel guests and town dignitaries had gathered. The hotel manager made introductions. I made myself smile.

Ma had saved a chair next to her at a long oblong table. She must have anticipated that hunger would drive me downstairs eventually, because there was plate of food in front of my chair to match her own.

Ma was answering questions between bites of roast beef, potatoes, and peas. I tried to eat, but my throat closed against food.

As I looked around the room, I wondered what secrets lurked in the hearts below every starched collar and prim cameo. I tried out my would-have-been name again. Clara O'Keeffe. How would Clara O'Keeffe be different from Clara Estby? Which parts of me were from Ma and the father I had never met and which were the result of how I had lived and the choices I had made?

"How many pairs of shoes have you worn out?" someone asked.

"Have you ever been lost?"

"Do you think you'll make it to New York in time to win your bet?"

Over the last one hundred interviews, Ma had developed scripted answers to entertain our listeners and make herself look intelligent and resourceful. I had heard it all.

I guess she hadn't completely forgotten about me, though, because at the question "What did you bring with you?" she reached over to hold my hand before she enumerated the contents of our satchels.

I gripped the stair railing on the way back to our room, still lightheaded with thoughts of a stranger father. Ma gave me a one-armed hug as we entered our room and was asleep in five minutes.

I knew I wouldn't sleep, so there was no point in going to bed. I found my journal and sat by the window, trying to write by the light of the street lamps below. What was I really upset about? That Ma wasn't perfect? I knew that already. That Pa wasn't my father? If anything I loved him more, for taking me on and treating me as his own when he didn't have to.

For a minute, maybe two, I was so angry at Ma that I was tempted to desert her. But the sensible thing to do would be to put every ounce of willpower behind winning the bet. If I got even a quarter of the winnings I'd have enough to go to college and set up on my own anywhere in the country. But even if I wanted to cut myself off from Ma and her endless demands, did I want to cut myself off from Pa and Ida and all the rest? It was too much to work out tonight.

A clock outside struck one, then two. If we had to walk at least eight hours tomorrow—today now—I had to get a few hours' sleep. I slipped into bed next to Ma and tried to empty my mind by concentrating on the *clop-clop* of horses on the streets two floors down. At last, I stopped hearing hoofbeats, or anything else.

The next morning, I got up before Ma was awake and took a bath and washed my hair. A private bathroom—even Nellie Bly had not traveled any better than this. My shorter hair was already starting to dry, and I whirled my head from side to side, enjoying the feeling of my hair's freedom as it brushed my cheeks.

At least my moods did not last for months, like Ma's. I had already regained my equilibrium and was ready to do what I had to do, which was get Ma to New York. After that? Maybe I'd start a new life in New York—go to college there, even change my name. No one would have to know anything about me except what I told them.

Ma sat up as I came out of the bathroom. "What happened to your hair?" She scrambled out of bed to take a closer look.

"I think I'll like it," I said. "It just needs to be evened up a bit."

She held out uneven chunks, grimacing. "It looks like it got caught in the egg beater and you cut it out with a paring knife."

"Close," I said. "Arthur's penknife."

"If you wanted shorter hair, you should have waited until we had proper scissors, or until we had the money to take you to a barber shop."

"I should have waited? That should have been your motto." This morning I said it with humor I could not have mustered last night. "If I occasionally act impetuously, at least I know where that came from, don't I?"

At first Ma bristled at the reference to last night's revelation; then she sighed with resignation. "If Patrick and I had married when I found out about you, he would have had to get a job instead of finishing college..." Ma twisted her wedding band. "If we had married...I often wondered if he would have resented me, resented you, for taking away his chance at college. And Ole loves you because you brought him and me together, which was what he had secretly wanted but never dared to hope for. So maybe my guardian angel did the right thing after all.

"Well," she said as she stretched, "done's done. I tried to imagine how Ole felt, with his wife moony and red-eyed, belly swollen with someone else's child. That's when I decided to stop fussing about not having the man I thought would make me happy and worry more about making happy the man who had been willing to take me on."

She started to unbraid her hair. "My turn for a bath."

From the firm set of her mouth, I guessed Ma wasn't going to add more to what she had already said. She had just taken away everything I thought I knew about myself, and the very floor felt fragile, as if it might collapse at my next step.

"This is hard for me, too," Ma said, "but we could argue a thousand years and say a million words and it wouldn't change anything. Can we agree not to talk about it anymore?"

At my dismayed look, Ma held me tight, so tight that I could feel her heart beating rapidly against mine. "I'm not the easiest mother, am I?" she said as she pulled back, then leaned forward to kiss my forehead.

December 7, 1896

Dear Mr. Doré,

Thanks to you, I will never forget my nineteenth birthday. Ma will not be any more jubilant at winning $10,000 than I was at receiving that $5.00 from Street and Smith, through the good agency of my esteemed correspondent, Mr. Charles Doré. I was also impressed with your research skills. To think that from Salt Lake City you could get details of an inconsequential birth record for someone born all those years ago!

Again, many thanks for your efforts on my behalf to publish my first story.

> *Sincerely,*
> *Miss Clara Estby*

CHAPTER 27

AN URGENT MESSAGE

December 13, 1896—Day 222

Coal country, Pennsylvania

WITH THREE days before our December 16 deadline, we were still zigzagging through hills and more hills in Pennsylvania. We were too far behind schedule to stop and earn money, so each morning I ripped newspapers into three-inch squares to layer over the holes in the bottom of my worn-out boots. Despite stabbing cold and slippery footing, we started walking while it was still dark and we walked until I felt like I was no longer a person but a machine someone had fired up and forgot to turn off. I was tired unto tears.

I felt the trembling earth beneath my feet as coal cars rumbled by. The rhythm of our steps pounded in my head. I wanted to curl up in front of someone's fireplace and sleep. But I didn't want Ma saying I'd spoiled our chances of winning because I was mad at her or gave up. To have a chance at winning that ten thousand dollars I was willing to walk until we froze dead in our tracks or reached New York.

December 14, 1896 – Day 223
Hummelstown, Pennsylvania

I wasn't just tired. I was sick. While my forehead burned, my eyes stung in freezing air. I was just trying to decide if the sky looked like more snow when I stepped on an icy patch that sent my feet and head in opposite directions. I hit the ground in a belly flop, with my right ankle bent awkwardly. I weakly slapped the ice I lay on. We were due in New York the day after tomorrow, and the only way we'd get there by then was if Ma's guardian angel swooped down and flew us there. The last seven and a half months would have been for nothing.

Ma silently lifted me into a stand and I draped my left arm over her shoulder.

"*Ish da, ish da,*" I muttered along with each step as I hobbled, entwined with Ma, a long mile to the next rail stop.

I was too miserable to care what station we sat in.

"I wouldn't have wished it on you, but maybe your bad ankle is our reprieve," Ma said.

"Another extension?" I croaked.

Ma had been dragging the last few days, but the possibility of a new deadline put an optimistic spark back in her eye. "How much time should I ask for?" Ma said.

I pressed my palms to my temples to subdue the throbbing while I figured. We had one hundred and twenty-eight more miles through Pennsylvania, and at least sixty-five across New Jersey to where we'd take the ferry to New York. Our old deadline gave us two days, and we needed a minimum of eight. I was afraid to ask for more; Miss Waterson might turn us down. "We need at least six more days," I said.

"It shouldn't matter," Ma said. "I was the one who asked for a deadline, to add a little hoopla to our venture. But I'll ask for six days."

"We should have proof that we notified her that we were entitled to an extension. But how can we write a letter and get a response in two days?" I said.

Looking through the window, I saw a row of icicles hanging from the eaves like Christmas tree decorations and an ice-encased line swooping up from the side of the station to the telegraph pole beside the tracks. "How much does a telegram cost?" I said.

Half an hour later, I was propped up on a bench in the waiting room with a bandanna packed with crushed icicles on my ankle while we waited for a reply from New York. The railroad men had come to our rescue again. They telegraphed our message to the New York station, which relayed it to Western Union, where they took up a collection to have it delivered to Miss Waterson. Our message was brief:

```
Illness and sprained ankle (stop)
New deadline Dec 22
```

If Miss Waterson agreed, we had eight days instead of two to get to New York.

Three-thirty, four o'clock. Four-thirty. Four-thirty-seven. The minutes ticked by without an answer. Every half hour or so, someone in the waiting room would knock down fresh icicles for my ankle. Finally, at five o'clock, we gave up on getting an answer that day.

One of the railway men helped us to his family's home. The next morning there was a reply from New York, but it was from Western Union, not Miss Waterson.

```
Message delivered (stop)
Addressee declined to answer
```

No answer. Did that mean she had refused to agree to an extension? Did she think we had made up an illness? Did she suspect we had exaggerated the time I needed to recover? Or by not contesting our claim for an extension, had she assumed we understood that she accepted it?

December 15, 1896 – Day 224
Near Hummelstown, Pennsylvania

We packed up before dawn. I iced my ankle one more time, and gratefully accepted a gnarled wood cane from the people we stayed with last night—another family from the list of recommendations from the suffragists we met clear back in Des Moines. My cheeks burned and my head was so stuffed that I thought it might burst my skull, but I was still willing to crawl the last two hundred miles to get to New York on time. After a grueling mile, I wanted to be back in bed. Ma didn't seem to notice my limp and bleary eyes. I was also miffed that she seemed to think that once she'd told me about my real father, that was the end of it.

Ma called a halt as we came to a park bench under a bare oak tree within a stone's toss of a creek that ran through the village.

"Even if we walk from dawn to midnight, we may miss our deadline." Ma cleared her throat and leaned toward me to whisper, "We could sneak a ride on a train to make up lost time. The hoboes do it all the time."

"But Miss Waterson said she had spies watching us!"

Ma looked behind her, under the bench, and up in the trees. "I don't see any spies. Do you?"

"No..."

She sagged against the back of the bench and lifted her

chin so all she could see was sky. Was she looking for her guardian angel? Maybe she had been affected by what she'd told me in Pittsburgh, even if she didn't want to talk about it. She drew her feet up under her skirt on the bench as she turned to me. "Why should you cripple yourself just so we can say we walked all the way to New York by some artificial deadline?"

I couldn't read her face. Was she giving up, or goading me into disagreeing with her and pushing even harder toward New York? There was no way Ma and I could walk all the way home again, though. We had to keep going for any chance of getting the ten thousand dollars and a ride home in a first-class train car.

Grimly, I leaned over to unlace my boot, wrapped my bandanna tightly around my ankle, and snugged up the laces. "Let's go." Once we reached the border into New Jersey, we only had another sixty-odd miles to New York City.

Sunday, December 20, 1896—Day 228

Bethlehem, Pennsylvania

I had to confess we had missed church more than a few Sundays since we left Mica Creek. If we weren't walking, we were working for the next pair of shoes or sleeping. But this was nearly Christmas, and here we were in Bethlehem—Pennsylvania. This morning's Bible reading was the passage about the wise men.

During the sermon, I propped up my bad ankle on the kneeling rail and let my mind wander to the three wise men heading out into the desert to follow a star. How would I know when I got to the right place for my life without a star to guide me? Ma said I should feel lucky to have more choices than she had had, but having too many choices put me into a mugwumping dither. Bad choices now would lead to a life of misery. It was hard to make a living as a writer — a five-dollar check every month or two was not enough to live on. Shouldn't I do what most women did and marry? Or if I didn't marry, shouldn't I have another career to fall back on? But what career? Going through the alphabet didn't help: *A*, actress (too shy); *B*, ballet dancer (too tall); *C*, clerk (too boring); *D*, dentist (too frightening); *E*, engineer (too hard).

By the end of the sermon, I still didn't know what to do, and I found myself clutching Pa's owl so tightly that the beak had dented my palm.

After church, the congregation adjourned to the social hall. As I brushed off the crumbs of my fourth cookie (I hoped no one had been counting), I studied Ma. She had given up a life of private schools and parlors and married a man she did not love at first for my sake. She had served a ten-year sentence in a sod house, bringing forth a new child every other year. She was risking her life to save the farm that kept us from starving. And perhaps she knew that my future lay far beyond Mica Creek, and wanted this last year with me before I left to find my place in the bigger world. What more could she have done?

CHAPTER 28

CROSSING THE HUDSON

December 21, 1896—Day 230

Phillipsburg, on the western edge of New Jersey

ALL WE had to do to win now was walk eighteen hours out of the next thirty-six. No matter how much my ankle hurt, I could do that, couldn't I?

We paused on the station platform, still puffing steam like locomotives in the cold air, and looked out at the four sets of tracks leading out of Phillipsburg. Ma caught a station attendant by the elbow after he had helped an elderly woman up the steps to her railroad car. "Which line goes to New York?" she asked.

"This Lehigh line will get you there, and you just have time to get a ticket," he said. "The next runs on the other lines aren't until late tonight or tomorrow."

We ignored the ticket window, picked up our bags, and headed out along the Lehigh line. For several hours we trod along the winding tracks between rocky flat-topped ridges to the Three Bridges Station. We stamped our feet (or at least my good foot) in front of the little wood stove in the station house, peeled off our frost-stiffened gloves, and turned front sides and backsides to the fire.

When we could feel our toes again, we walked over to the New Jersey map posted on one wall and traced our day's walk. Ma blanched.

"That can't be right!" I leaned heavily on my cane as I leaned forward to check our route again, hoping we had misinterpreted the map. But no matter how many times I looked and recalculated, the answer was the same: we should have ignored the station attendant. He assumed we were taking a train to New York. Because of schedules, the Lehigh train would make it to New York before the other train lines, but on foot, the other routes were nearly twenty miles shorter. Walking in snow and ice, that extra twenty miles would take us at least seven extra hours — seven hours we could not spare.

We avoided looking at each other as we picked up our bags.

"Miss Waterson will still honor the contract." I meant to sound reassuring, but my voice trembled and floated upward as I spoke, turning the statement into a plaintive question. Desperation squeezed my throat like the noose around a condemned man's neck. "Surely she doesn't care if we arrive today or next week, as long as we show we can walk the distance by ourselves like we said we would." My throat was too pinched to continue. Ma did not answer.

We walked on the rest of the day and into the night.

December 22, 1896 – Day 231, our revised deadline
Newark, New Jersey

From Bound Brook, we followed the eastern edge of the Watchung Mountains to Plainfield. The sky had been brilliant blue earlier in the day, but by four o'clock it had turned dark and the temperature dropped at least ten degrees. I continued to limp along behind Ma to Newark. Electric streetcars passed us several times a minute on Market Street. I envied the shop and factory girls sitting down inside the cars on their way home.

According to the thermometer outside a hardware store it was twenty-four degrees. Squealing loads of children dragged their heels to stop their sleds at the bottom of a gentle hill perpendicular to the street we trod. Their joy was not contagious.

When we heard a forecast for northern gales and more snow, Ma wanted to stop in Newark but I persuaded her to go on. After a mile of breaking trail through fresh snow, we gave up and found a family to take us in.

Early morning, Wednesday,

December 23–Day 232

Still in Newark

❧

I was awake when the clock struck eleven. I was still awake when the clock tolled midnight. We had missed our deadline. But if the deadline was a part of the contract Ma had suggested in the first place to add drama to our trek, why should Miss Waterson care when we got there? That's probably why she hadn't bothered to answer our wire. I was sure of it. At least I convinced myself that I was sure enough of it that at last, despite a throbbing ankle and niggling doubts, I could sleep.

At six o'clock, I woke and sat up on the couch to look out the window. *"Ish da,"* I whispered. Fine dry snow was piling in drifts against the house. *"Ish da,"* I said again as I lay back down. Of course Miss Waterson would look for any excuse not to part with ten thousand dollars, and with this additional snow we would miss our deadline not by minutes, but most of a day — and that was assuming she'd granted us the extra six days for my ankle. Well, it would be madness to give up now, when we were just a short walk and a river away from Manhattan. We'd cross our fingers.

Half an hour later, bundled against the biting wind, we headed toward Jersey City. We counted out money for tickets

and found standing room on the ferry among farmers with bra-
ziers on wheels loaded with roasted potatoes and poultry men
with horse-drawn wagons loaded with boxes of Christmas geese
and chickens. We all struggled to keep our footing as the ferry
dipped and rocked in the wind-roughened river.

CHAPTER 29

MISS WATERSON

Wednesday, December 23, 1896—Day 232
New York City, New York

W E BUMPED to a stop at the pier, and
while deck hands tied the ferry to cleats
we joined other foot passengers walking
down the gangplank. If Ma was expecting a
welcoming committee, she was disappointed.
Truth to tell, I was disappointed, too.

We didn't rate a brass band, but New York
greeted us with its own natural self. I went
giddy with the overstimulation to my senses.
Every breath brought in the musty smell of the
river, coal smoke, hot sausage, and chestnuts; my
ears rang with the competing sounds of rattling streetcars with
squealing brakes, strains of carols from a Salvation Army band,
hawkers' cries in every accent and language, wagon wheels, and

horses' hooves. We tripped over darting dogs and feral cats, dodged between restless cart horses and people of every color crowding onto streetcars, carrying bundles of garments, all in a hurry. At every intersection, the whistle of a traffic policeman cut through the noise to keep the tangle of vehicles and pedestrians from colliding into a logjam that even Paul Bunyan could not have sorted out.

One minute I was ready to clamber on a bench, wave my cane in the air, and shout to all passersby: "We did it! We walked all the way from Mica Creek to New York City!" The next minute I was ready to empty what was left of my breakfast into the nearest trash can, so sick I was with the suspense of wondering whether Miss Waterson would honor our bet. "Get out your map, Ma. Let's find Miss Waterson's office." I wanted to get it over with.

"I can't believe there was no one here to welcome us," Ma said. Her voice was tight with tension. I guessed she meant Miss Waterson as well as her fans, and feared today might not go as she hoped it would.

"You can't expect folks to wait around in the snow all day for you, Ma. Miss Waterson is probably staying warm in her office," I said. I hoped I was right.

Crossing Broadway, we dodged a horse-drawn double-decker bus. The clock in the domed cupola of City Hall read 1:03 p.m., thirteen hours and three minutes after our revised deadline.

As we stared at the clock, an urchin rammed Ma's back and yanked her satchel out of her hand. He darted through the crowd, faster than a jackrabbit, up the broad sidewalk ahead of us.

"Stop! Thief!" we howled, and ran (well, Ma ran; I limped far behind) screaming, slipping, and bumping into people as we tried to catch him. Before the end of the block, he had disappeared.

We stood, panting, looking in the direction of the thief.

"Ish da!" I wailed.

Ma's face drooped. "Our last two dollars and thirty-two cents, two hundred pages of notes, my curling iron."

I put my arm around Ma's shoulder, barely aware of the throngs parting to glide on around us. "You must have sent two thousand pages of notes home by now, and I have my journal, too. You can still write the book."

Ma compressed her lips and continued to look in the direction that cutpurse had fled.

As we continued to walk toward Miss Waterson's office, Ma flexed her arm as if she could not get used to walking without the familiar weight of her satchel in her hand. Welcome to New York City! Both carrying satchels and gawking like the small-town folks we were—we had been an easy target. I hoped he'd enjoy Ma's curling iron and sliver of soap left from the hotel in Pittsburgh.

I lifted my chin and took a deep breath of crisp air. We might have started in a small town, but I'd bet most of the folks bustling by us on the sidewalks hadn't seen as much of the country as we had. And maybe in an hour we'd be richer than most of the people passing us by. Despite my ankle, I encouraged Ma to a brisker pace. We elbowed our passage on crowded sidewalks two blocks south on Broadway to John, east on John to William, and left to find 95. On side streets muffled by rows of tall buildings, the sounds of Broadway blended to a hum. My breathing quieted sufficiently to hear the muffled foghorns and ferry whistles from the river. A squirrel dashed across our path, and a gray storm of pigeons swirled up off the sidewalk at our approach.

At 95 William Street, we opened the lobby door, almost bumping our heads on a bare light bulb dangling from the ceiling. Since the bulb wasn't burning, the narrow flight of stairs was lit only by the fading natural light seeping through smudged windows on either side of the entry door. On the landing, one door read: P. L. MITCHUM, ATTORNEY-AT-LAW; the other read: A. J. WATERSON, PUBLISHER. What would happen when we finally passed through the door to the mysterious Miss Waterson?

Ma smoothed her hair, squared her shoulders, and rapped. I willed my heart to beat silently as I strained my ears for any sound from the other side of Miss Waterson's door, but there was silence, only silence. The handle turned when Ma tried it, so we entered on tiptoe, feeling like trespassers. No one sat at the small oak desk, which was clear save for a ledger, ink bottle, and tray of pens. Oak filing cabinets lined a side wall, and another door punctuated the back wall. Was it the door to Miss Waterson's private office? I alternately fanned and clenched my fingers as I crossed the room, resolutely raised my hand, and knocked.

A chair scraped and heavy footsteps approached the door. "Who's there?" The voice — was it Miss Waterson's? — sounded suspicious, surprised, and annoyed. I stepped back nervously as the door opened a crack to reveal a vertical slice of fleshy cheek and one dark eye. The door started to close.

"Wait," Ma said. She thrust one booted toe into the narrowing crack and held up her calling card. "I'm Helga Estby, the woman who walked here from Spokane!"

A long-fingered, bony hand reached through the crack and plucked the card from Ma, then withdrew, leaving the door ajar. As we entered, the woman retreated to the far side of room behind a battered desk.

She was an inch or so taller than Ma, with lusterless brown hair pulled back loosely in a mouse-nest bun. She wore a threadbare, gored black skirt with a black shawl and high-necked shirtwaist. While she read Ma's card over the top of her glasses, I read the nameplate on her desk: Astilbe Jasmine Waterson. She looked more like a prickly thistle than a feathery astilbe.

Miss Waterson tossed Ma's card on the desk. "How unfortunate that you missed your deadline by nearly a week after walking so far."

Ma steadied herself on the arm of a chair. "We're less than a day late!"

"You didn't even answer our telegram," I said.

"You can't expect me to waste money on a telegram, can you?" she said.

"Ish da," I moaned.

A pink flush spread from beneath Miss Waterson's high collar and mottled her cheeks. Her body was ramrod stiff, but one finger on her left hand fluttered against her worn, dark skirt. She was obviously nervous, too, so maybe she was just trying to bluff us out of our money and could be convinced to change her mind. I turned to Ma. She could talk anybody into anything.

"It wasn't our fault!" Ma protested. "Someone gave us bad directions, and we walked fifty miles out of our way in a snowstorm."

"I suppose God had His reasons for preventing you from meeting the conditions of your contract," Miss Waterson answered.

When Ma's face turned moist and bread-dough pale, I settled her securely in the chair before she fainted. I had counted on Ma to argue down Miss Waterson if she had to, but Ma clearly wasn't up to it. But why did I have to rely on Ma to do my talking for me? With Norwegian courage and Irish blarney in my blood, I should be a match for Miss Waterson. After all, I had slept among the Indians, shot a highwayman, and talked to President-Elect McKinley himself. Why should one ordinary, unarmed woman have me tongue-tied? I looked Miss Waterson in the eye and filled my lungs.

"Miss Waterson, we walked from Mica Creek to New York, just like we said we would. We honored the contract and have kept your name a secret until now. But if you don't pay us the ten thousand dollars, we'll tell the *New York World* that

Astilbe Jasmine Waterson turned those valiant women walkers out into the snow just before Christmas."

Miss Waterson opened her mouth to speak, but I was just getting warmed up. "One hundred years from now people will still be calling anyone who's as mean-hearted as you a 'Waterson.' They will say Scrooge was a kindly soul next to you. Is that how you want to be remembered?"

Miss Waterson frowned and turned to look out the window, hands knotted behind her back. Three times she rose on her toes and settled back down on her heels before she turned back to face us. "Here's a compromise." She unlocked her desk drawer and withdrew a tin box.

I counted the money as she laid it out: a five-dollar bill, four ones, two quarters, three dimes, two nickels, and ten pennies. "Ten dollars!"

Miss Waterson drew her loosely knit shawl higher on her shoulders and fingered the safety pin that held her shawl in place. "That's as much as you started with."

Ten dollars. Was that all seven and a half months of danger, exhaustion, and privation was worth?

"Besides that ten dollars, you can also have a share of the profits after I've made back my expenses on publishing the book." She extended her large-knuckled hand like a greedy child reaching for the last piece of chocolate on the plate. "Do you have your journals with you?"

"No!" I said. "And even if we did we wouldn't give them to you." I knew I should be strong, but I felt like a child who had just been told that Christmas had been canceled this year. I could not keep the petulance from my voice. "Why did you even make the bet if you didn't mean to keep it?"

"I thought it was safe to agree to the ten thousand dollars your mother asked for, because the chances were you'd never make it all the way. You could make a little money giving lectures on your adventures as far as you went, and I would get publicity for a book I could help you write."

"But when you read the newspaper accounts, you saw we were stubborn enough to keep going. Why didn't you tell us to stop? We almost died in the lava fields and the flash flood…" I waited for Miss Waterson to defend herself, but she said nothing.

"Do you have any idea what Ma and I went through to get here, day after day?" I stared at Miss Waterson with the intensity of a Colorado rattler.

I plopped on the floor and hoisted my right foot over my left knee. *"Ish da, ish da,"* I muttered as my hands, shaking with cold and rage, fumbled with my bootlaces.

"Clara…" For the first time on this trip, it was Ma who looked embarrassed by something I was doing.

I ignored her as I jerked loose sections of my worn laces from the eyelets and flung each shredded remnant toward Miss Waterson's desk. I yanked down the tongue of my boot and winced as I eased the boot past my swollen ankle. I peeled off two layers of socks, leaned back on my hands, and held up my battered foot.

"Look at this foot. How many miles a day do you walk? Two miles, three? When we weren't working for the next pair of boots, we walked twenty-five, thirty, fifty miles a day, sometimes with no food, day after day, for two hundred and thirty-two days." I jabbed my foot toward Miss Waterson, daring her to ignore the missing toenails, purple-splotched ankle, and horse-hoof calluses.

I pointed back at Ma, still slumped in the chair. "Ma left seven children at home for nearly eight months to earn that ten thousand dollars. We were counting on that money to save the farm! She has ruined her health, and baby Lillian and little William may not even remember their Ma by the time we get home."

Miss Waterson glanced at my mangled foot. "Don't blame all your troubles on me," she said. "I didn't make your mother set up this wager. I just agreed to it and made sure she kept to the stipulations she established herself." She looked anywhere but my eyes.

I scooped up the ten dollars from her desk, slipped my laceless boot back on, hobbled over to Ma, and half carried her down the stairs, muttering every epithet I could think of. "Execrable scoundrel. Boil-covered blackguard. Fork-tongued fiend."

CHAPTER 30

WE HAD A STORY TO TELL

W E PASSED the post office on the way back toward the World Building. Ma's satchel was stolen; we were denied the money we'd earned—yes, earned—by walking nearly four thousand miles, I felt like screaming, but the post office was no place for a tantrum. During the hour I had to wait in line for our mail, I couldn't help muttering angrily to myself. Other customers kept their distance. Ma did, too. She leaned against the wall near the door, well out of my range.

I put the letters in the pocket inside my coat, and as we left the post office I switched my satchel to the hand closest to Ma. "Keep your hand on it, too, Ma."

She didn't speak, but I felt her hand snug up against mine on the handle. No thief would get our remaining worldly goods.

We continued on up Fulton to Broadway, where it joined Park Row. There in an imperial line were the buildings that housed offices for the *New York Times, Tribune, Herald, Sun,* and the *New York World.* Millions of words, every day, originated in those very buildings and were shipped all over the world. Nellie Bly, girl reporter, might have walked this very sidewalk on the way to work. Ma's footsteps continued to slow. I pulled on the satchel to keep her moving. At least it would be warm inside.

I expected to see a bustling newsroom when we opened the door to the New York World building, but the main floor was just a lobby, surrounded by business offices. We stood for a moment, irresolute. With more confidence than I felt, I pointed toward six uniformed men standing at attention in front of a row of elevators and said, "Come on, Ma. One of those men will know where to go."

An operator ushered us into a paneled elevator and shut the doors. I could hardly breathe as I watched the floor indicator edge toward twelve. We lurched as the elevator halted, then jerked as he pulsed the lever through the last five inches to line up with the floor. Then he opened the grill and outer doors and offered a white-gloved hand to escort Ma across the threshold.

The men in the newsroom seemed more interested in swapping jokes, spitting tobacco, and imbibing who knew what from various bottles littering the desks than finding out who had just walked through their doors, but I was still riled up about how Miss Waterson had treated us and wanted someone to listen. I pried the satchel out of Ma's hands and let it drop with a *thunk* on the nearest desk. No one paid any attention. I clapped my hands like a schoolmistress calling a rowdy class to order. "Who wants a good story?" I called.

One reporter broke away from his cronies and strolled toward us. "What's the scoop?"

"My mother and I have just walked from Spokane, Washington, to New York City, and as soon as we got here we were robbed, and then the woman who promised us ten thousand dollars if we made it here refused us the money with the excuse that we were thirteen hours late!"

"So you're those women walkers," he said. "Didn't we run your picture when you just started out?" He ushered us into a glass-walled office out of the fray. "Nobody here thought you'd make it."

A year ago I wouldn't have believed we could do it, either.

He leaned out of the office. "Hey, somebody get Fineman!" he called.

"I'm Bill Lankowski," he said, turning back to us as we collapsed into chairs. He borrowed a notebook from the desk he had appropriated, propped himself against a wall, and scribbled frantically as I started to tell him everything that had happened in the last eight months since the *World* printed the first article about us.

I'd half dragged Ma from Miss Waterson's office to the newsroom, but Mr. Lankowski's attention began to infuse her with her old energy. She broke in to explain how she hoped our feat would demonstrate the resourcefulness and strength of women, and how passionately she supported women's suffrage.

He was more interested in the sixteen pairs of boots we'd each worn out, and whether I'd ever had to use my gun. Seeing that he wanted adventure and not politics, we recounted the time we had escaped jail in La Grande; how a penknife and scrap of rope had saved Ma's life in a flash flood; how we'd survived a blizzard in the Blues and the lava fields in Idaho; and how we'd camped with Indians and sipped tea with President-Elect McKinley and his wife.

We had done the walking, all eight million steps. But we hadn't done it unaided. I couldn't even remember the faces of everyone who had taken us in for a night, fed us, let us wash, left water by the tracks for us.

Ma was just relating how Miss Waterson had refused to pay us the ten thousand dollars, and how a ruffian had stolen her satchel when her voice faltered. Then, as if someone wound her spring again, she regained momentum. "Mr. Lankowski, my daughter and I haven't eaten in days and we walked fifty miles in a blizzard after being given bad directions. If we don't get something to eat and a place to stay tonight, we're going to expire right here." She slumped in her chair and sighed. How many times had I cringed as Ma shamelessly finagled our next bed or meal? This time I was grateful. Mr. Lankowski fetched two cups of water and gathered morsels from the plates and bowls of snacks scattered around the outer workroom.

Popcorn, pretzels, pickles, and peanuts were a bad combination. After a few bites I pushed my plate away and watched the sketch artist, Mr. Fineman, arrange his sketchpad, ink, and pens on the desk. After conferring with Mr. Lankowski, he asked us to stand and look in the same direction while I held out my gun.

"I don't want millions of people to see me as a desperado," I said.

"How about extending one arm, then, as if pointing something out to your mother?" he said.

A few minutes later, Mr. Fineman put down his pen. "Got it," he said.

I dropped my arm and stepped over to his sketchpad to see if his portrait flattered me. "You can't do that," I sputtered, jabbing a finger at the daggers and pistols he'd put in both Ma's hands and mine.

Before I could complain about how he had turned a penknife into pirate daggers and one small pistol into two six-guns, Mr. Fineman gathered his supplies and scuttled off to have his sketch engraved for tomorrow's paper.

Mr. Lankowski shrugged apologetically. "Guns and daggers sell newspapers," he said. "Here, I'll make it up to you." He beckoned us to follow, selected a key from a hook, and led us down the back stairwell to the eleventh floor. "I'm sure Mr. Pulitzer wouldn't want the subjects of my story to sleep in the snow," he said, looking over his shoulder.

He opened one of the doors in a long hallway and led us

into a combination apartment and office. "It's one of the rooms we camp out in when we're working late on assignment, but even Scrooge wouldn't expect us all to work late over Christmas. I'll tell the caretaker you'll be here a couple days."

After demonstrating the lights and gas ring for tea, he gave us leave to use paper and stamps from the desk and eat any food we found in the cupboard. Just as he opened the door to leave, he turned. "Most important," he said, blushing slightly and pointing down the hall. "Convenience and bathing tub on the left. It's the door with no room number." The door almost closed, then popped open again. "And Merry Christmas!"

The door closed with a click and we were alone in New York City.

CHAPTER 31

LETTERS

WITHOUT the distractions of Miss Waterson and the newsroom, I was acutely aware of my throbbing ankle. I could feel every heartbeat in it, and I should have taken a chair and put my feet up, but I was too restless to sit. I limped around the room, poking into every drawer and cupboard like a curious cat. The dresser held a clean set of men's underdrawers, laundered shirt, and fresh collar. The cupboard by the sink had tinned soup, tea, soda crackers, half a loaf of hard bread that had not yet turned green, and a few dishes. A typing machine perched on the desk; the drawer below had paper, envelopes, stamps, a ruler, and paper clips.

Eleven floors above the street and all its sounds, the apartment seemed unnaturally quiet.

Then my anger at Miss Waterson erupted again, and I hurled my hat toward the bed. "I thought Miss Waterson was a friend of one of your suffrage society women! No friend would treat us the way Miss Waterson did."

Ma swallowed and crossed her fists protectively against her chest. "Miss Waterson wasn't—exactly—a friend of one of my Spokane friends. One woman in my group did suggest getting a publisher to sponsor the walk, though. So I wrote with my plan to a few publishers, and Miss Waterson took me up on it."

"A few?"

"A dozen or so. Maybe more." Ma averted her eyes.

I thought of all the stamps and paper Ma had gone through this spring. "How many more?" I raised my eyebrows and waited for the real number.

Ma sighed a put-upon sigh. "All the publishers listed in the New York City telephone directory."

I looked to the ceiling for divinely inspired forbearance. "You risked our lives on a bet with the only person in New York City willing to take you up on it? Miss Waterson had nothing to lose. If we won, she'd just admit she didn't have the money. If we lost—which she was sure we would—she'd still have publicity for the book you two would write and you'd both get rich."

I scooped up Miss Waterson's money from my pocket and flung it on the bed. "There's no helping fools and idiots!" I counted myself among that number. All we had to show for seven months and eighteen days on the road was ten dollars—part of it in nickels and dimes—and my five-dollar check from Street and Smith. In April I had had thirty-seven dollars and forty-eight cents in my college fund. That left us twenty-two dollars and forty-eight cents behind where we started.

While Ma wilted down on the bed, I plopped down on the straight chair by the desk. Easing my boot over my swollen ankle, I set off throbbing I could feel from my toenails to my eyeballs. Still sitting, I struggled out of my overcoat, heavy with melted snow, and draped it behind me, over the back of my chair. I knew Ma sometimes believed in her fancies so hard that they became true — for her. At least until times like now, when her fancies collided with reality. Why hadn't I questioned her more about Miss Waterson and how the bet came about before we left? Maybe I had wanted to believe her fancies, too.

Perhaps there was good news in the mail. I fished our letters out of my inside coat pocket and hobbled over to the bed to place Pa's letter, along with those from my brothers and sisters, on Ma's lap. I poked at the money on the bed. Maybe some other publisher in New York would pay us enough for our story to get us back home and save the farm.

I had letters from Charles Doré and Erick Iverson, but I didn't want to know what either of them had to say. Mr. Doré was just probably writing to tell me when he was going to marry Miss Ernestine. Erick would be writing to say he'd been smitten by sister Ida's cherry pies and decided to marry her if he couldn't have me. *Uff da!* I tossed both letters on the bed. I wasn't going to be like a woman trapped in a Jane Austen novel, preoccupied only with who was going to marry whom.

By now, Ma had crawled under the blankets and propped herself up against the headboard and pillows so she could stare out the window. Blue bruiselike circles had blossomed under her eyes again. I crawled in with her and stretched one arm around her shoulders. As the foot trod we were nearly four thousand miles from home, and Christmas was the day after tomorrow.

As I leaned my head against hers, I was reminded of the night we'd spent on the ledge above the flood, wrapped around each other. We had survived the flood, and we would survive New York City. For a night or two, we had a bed, blankets, and food. Compared to what else we'd been through this year, this room was luxury.

As I squeezed Ma's shoulder, she roused herself. "I'm sorry, Clara." Her voice was as raspy as it had been after three days in the lava fields. "After all this we'll go home empty-handed. We'll still lose the farm...Were we wrong to go?"

In my usual mugwumping way, I had a thousand reasons to say yes but at least a reason or two to say no. My stomach cramped. I needed food to settle my stomach. "Let's eat. Then we'll talk." I slid out of bed and opened the tin of soup, found a pan, and lit the gas ring. While the soup heated, I limped over to the desk and slid the typewriter over to make room for bowls, spoons, and a plate of crackers. I propped the letters up on the paper carriage on the typewriter. For Ma's sake, I hoped at least some of it was good news.

As I dished up soup, its steam made my eyes water. We ate slowly and silently.

Ma put her spoon down gently, aligning it carefully in a ninety-degree angle with the edge of the desk. She looked out the window. "How can I face Pa without the money?"

Even in profile I could tell Ma was showing her age. Although her face was so gaunt that her cheekbones stuck out like crab apples, the line of her throat was beginning to sag. And when had the hair at her temples gone gray?

"Pa will just be happy to see you home safely, Ma." I pulled Pa's letter from the stack and held it toward her.

Her open hand hesitated for a heartbeat above the letter before closing on it. She read aloud:

December 17, 1896

Dear Mrs. Estby,

I hope you are sitting down when you read this because I have taken a drastic step. I took no news as bad news, and assumed you missed your deadline. I sold all our farm equipment and our plow horse to Erick Iverson. He paid me more than I expected, enough to make partial payments on both the mortgage and the taxes. The bank and the county treasurer have said they'll give us another year before auctioning off the farm.

I can hear you saying, "How will we grow wheat without the equipment?" Well, we won't. We've lost money on the wheat the last three years anyway. We'll just plant a little hay the old-fashioned way, by hand, work our kitchen garden and orchard, and keep the milk cow, pigs, and chickens to feed the family.

If we're meant to keep the farm, Providence will provide.

*If we're not, we'd have to sell the equipment anyway, and now
we have a head start on it.*

We all miss you.

> *Your husband,*
> *Ole Estby*

Ma dropped the letter, mouth open, but wordless.

I snatched up the letter and used my skirt to wipe off a
splash of soup from one corner. I reread the letter. The farm
was still ours, at least for another year. My hand was shaking
as I put the letter back down on Ma's side of the desk. Ma
and I had walked nearly four thousand miles and were going
home broke. Pa walked across the road to sell some farm equipment and had saved the farm. At least for now. I fumbled in my
pocket for Pa's wise owl and perched it on the windowsill.

I supposed I should see what Erick had to say. I tapped his
letter on the table, nerving myself to open it. I slipped a table
knife under the flap, but the knife was dull and my hands were
still shaking. The envelope ripped down the front.

November 26, 1896

Dear Clara,

*Don't worry. I didn't take you at your word when you wrote
to say that you were refusing my proposal. Your walk across the
country has clearly drained all your reasoning capacity to fuel*

*your feet. I don't blame you—you were just going out of loy-
alty to your folks.*

    *To give you something happy to think on, I write to tell
you I have finished our bed and table and laid the foundation for
our house. It is a goodly twenty by twenty, and we can add to it
as our family grows. I suppose I should have waited until you
returned to get your opinion on where the sink should go and all,
but now that harvest is over I had to find something to keep busy
while I waited for you to come home.*

    *My brothers have warned me that too much time under the
influence of your mother would corrupt your modest, obliging
nature. I am convinced, however, that once you are safely home
you will be restored to your own sweet self.*

    With love,
    Erick Iverson

    *P.S. Happy birthday! Don't worry about the farm. I've
talked to my pa and we have a plan to help.*

Now what? I looked to Ma for advice, but she was smiling as she read her letters from Olaf, Ida, Bertha, Arthur, and
Johnny. I didn't want to spoil her mood by dithering about
whether I owed Erick anything for helping save the farm and
wailing about having wasted over half a year on a foolhardy
walk.

Was the half-year entirely wasted, though? Since I thought
better with a pencil in my hand, I got out my journal.

Across the top of one of the last blank pages I wrote: *Goals for the walk.*

Under goals, I wrote: *1. Save the farm.*

At least Ma had tried. Her plan hadn't worked, but it might have, if someone other than Miss Waterson had taken her up on her wager. We still had a story to sell to someone else. I tapped my pencil against my two front teeth.

"You know, Ma, maybe we didn't do so bad." I turned my journal around so she could read it. "Money from selling some of the farm equipment gives us another year. That's long enough for you to write your book."

"Who wants to read about losers?"

"We walked nearly coast to coast. That counts for something." Ma did not look convinced, but I went on.

"What else did you say you wanted this walk to do? Prove..." I paused to let Ma finish the statement.

Ma sighed. "Prove the endurance of women."

I wrote it down: *2. Prove the endurance of women.*

"Remember that *New York World* article that ended 'if they survive the experiment'? Well, we did survive. And I'll bet more than one woman reading about us was inspired to try something she wasn't bold enough to try before."

I didn't wait for Ma to give me the next reason, but wrote down: *3. VOTES for women.*

"Idaho passed its referendum giving women the vote just a few months after we passed through."

"I don't think we can take credit for that, Clara."

"No. But maybe we changed a few votes. If every woman who is passionate about equal suffrage wins just a few votes, and a few votes more, eventually we will win."

Next I wrote down: *4. Money for college.*

"Tea with McKinley, camping out with Indians, seeing the whole country nearly coast to coast on foot…think of the scholarship application letter I can write now! I'll probably have colleges fighting over me. That is, if you can spare me," I said.

Ma pulled her chair forward with a scrape. "You've done your duty to your family. Go to college. I'll feel guilty if you don't."

Only one unresolved issue. "Ma, Erick didn't believe me when I said I refused his proposal, and that's why he helped save the farm. Don't I owe him something?"

Ma looked at me like I was too stupid to be any child of hers. "You don't owe him your life, Clara. You told him no and he chose not to believe you. Besides, Erick got a good deal on that farm equipment. Your Pa always kept his tools in like-new condition, and Erick probably gave him less than fifty cents on the dollar for them."

"I've been thinking," she said. "Since you're the published writer in the family, why don't you write the book about the walk? You can have the notes I sent home. It's the least I can do after dragging you across the country."

"I'll put your name on it, too."

"I'd be proud. But your name should come first."

Again, Ma looked out at the snow drifting across the

window. This time it wasn't an empty stare. As she narrowed her eyes, I could tell she was thinking hard on something. She turned back with a grin. "I've got it—the title should be *Spokane to New York City, One Step at a Time.*"

"Our home is Mica Creek. It should be *Mica Creek to New York City.*"

"No one's heard of Mica Creek, and you could say our trip started when we left the office of the *Spokane Chronicle.*" Ma's pallor was slowly being replaced by spots of color.

We had plenty of time to argue about a title. I'd let Ma think she'd won—for now. I changed the subject. "Where should we start the book? Should I leave out the boring beginning with all the rain?" I asked.

"You have to put in the part about the man with the rifle, though," Ma said.

"And the lonesome stationmaster who needed his socks darned."

"Chopping wood."

"Eating grasshoppers."

"The Indians and the curling iron."

"The water bottles on the tracks."

Our momentum halted when Ma looked away, fiddling with the top button on her shirtwaist. I suspected she was remembering Pittsburgh. Passing time could not turn the evening she'd told me about my real father into a funny story or thrilling adventure. I suspected we would never talk about that night again. Ma turned back toward me with a question in her eyes. She would never ask for forgiveness, and I didn't feel she had to ask for it. I reached across the table and laid my hand on top of hers. "Love you, Ma," I said.

Her eyes welled up. She blinked. "Love you, Clara," she whispered.

I had this story to tell, but one book would not support me for the rest of my life. I thought about the wizened widow in Oregon, the stationmaster with holes in his socks, the dressmaker in Salt Lake City with her clothing store, Dr. Holmes in Wyoming, Mrs. Bryan, the McKinleys. I had passed through their lives for an hour, a day, and then moved on, but they all left parts of themselves in my mind. I couldn't help wonder what happened to them after we left. Maybe the father I'd never met would inspire a story, too. Nellie Bly didn't need a poetic imagination; she wrote about real people and places. I had a hundred people and places to write about, too.

And how about Mr. Doré's story? I pressed his letter against my chest and closed my eyes. I remembered his thick stubby eyelashes, the smell of his soap, the texture of his cheek against mine.

Dear Miss Estby,

Congratulations on reaching New York! Please write the very day you get there to let me know that you are well. I know you will have given interviews to the reporters at the World *and* Times *already, but I'd like to do an article about you and your*

mother, too, for the Deseret Evening News. *Would you write
me a page or two with what you most remember and places you'd
like to go back to?*

*I hope Salt Lake City is on your list of places to revisit.
I'll meet your train if you let me know when you expect to
arrive. Miss Ernestine would still like you to visit her class, but
don't do it on my account. I told her I planned to go to Seattle
and the Klondike next year to cover the gold strike. She told me
that if I went, I should not be surprised to find that she had
become engaged to someone else while I was gone.*

*While I was staying put in Salt Lake City learning the
newspaper business, you were off on your adventure, and now
perhaps you will put down roots long enough to go to college
while I go off adventuring. Do you suppose someday we'll be of
a mind to go adventuring or put down roots at the same time?*

*I will send you my address in Seattle as soon as I know it.
Travel home safely.*

> *Most sincerely yours,*
> *Charles Doré*

I slipped the letter between pages of my journal. A year
from now, after the excitement of the Klondike, would he
remember the gap-toothed girl who tromped into his office in
Salt Lake City?

How would my own story turn out? Related by blood or
not, I was Ole Estby's daughter: strong, stoic, reliable. Everyone
in Mica Creek said so. Perhaps I was also a little like the father
I had never met. I hoped I would also be like Ma, the brav-

est woman I knew, a woman who could envision a world better than the one she found herself in, where farm families kept their homes in bad times, where women could vote, and every child with the will could go to college.

In a lull between snow squalls, a shaft of late-afternoon light glinted silver off the lever on the typing machine. I stood in front of the desk. My right index finger hovered over the keys as I searched for the round black button with C for Clara. Most typists were men, but I could learn to type, too. I could support myself while I got started writing. I would write my own story day by day, one step at a time. If I just kept putting one foot in front of the other, I could go anywhere my dreams led me.

AUTHOR'S NOTE

CLARA AND HELGA ESTBY were real people, my great-aunt and great-grandmother. Newspaper articles documented their meetings with notables and described how they demonstrated their curling iron for a group of Indians and survived three days in the lava fields, a flash flood in the Rockies, mountain blizzards, rattlers, a cougar, and assailants. I hope Helga and Clara would not wince at the words I have put in their mouths or the thoughts I have put in their heads.

I made up Erick Iverson and Mr. Doré, and concocted a name for Clara's birth father, since Helga never revealed his name. Miss Waterson is also fiction, since no one knows who—if anyone—made the wager with Helga Estby. Helga said at first that it was with someone in the fashion industry, but later implied that it was someone in publishing. Although newspaper articles disagreed on many details, they all quote Helga's claim that she had a ten-thousand-dollar bet with a mysterious party in the East. In 1896, ten thousand dollars would have been thirty-five times what a typical unskilled woman worker would earn in a year. The payoff Helga claimed for the walk was so extravagant that I began to wonder if the ten-thousand-dollar figure was part of Helga's hoopla.

Helga was so inconsistent about other provisions of the contract and her deadlines that I even doubted if there was a contract, except in her lively imagination. Despite my doubts on the truth of the wager, I chose to stick to Helga's version of the story and cast Miss Waterson in the role of the "mysterious party."

This book ends with Helga and Clara expecting to sell their story for at least enough to save the farm. In real life, their story did not have a happy ending. They were left stranded in New York with no money, without a change of clothes.

With Clara's bad ankle, they could not have walked clear back across the country, especially not in winter. I imagine them walking across the new bridge to Brooklyn where there was a large Norwegian community and finding jobs scrubbing and cleaning—earning enough to keep them off the streets, but not enough to save for train fare home.

Spring came with bad news from Mica Creek. Clara's sister Bertha was dying of diphtheria. Helga and Clara were desperate to get back home. Someone hearing about their plight gave them railway tickets as far as Chicago. From Chicago they walked to Minneapolis, where newspapers printed long articles about them. With this publicity, they likely raised enough money to get the rest of the way home.

Back in Mica Creek, they were greeted with the news that

both Bertha and Johnny had died of diphtheria. Helga went into another of her dismal spells — the worst yet — and the family agreed never to talk about the trip again. Helga and Clara's journals and the letter with the signatures of all the famous people they met along the way were apparently destroyed.

Four years later they lost the farm, but moving to Spokane was not the disaster Helga had predicted. Her husband, Ole, later joined by Arthur (my father's father), started a construction business, which did well enough for the remaining family to have a comfortable home in Spokane. No one starved. Helga continued to demonstrate for women's suffrage and had her first chance to vote in a national election in 1920. She died in 1942.

And what of Clara? A year after the trip, Spokane businesswomen raised money for her to go to business school. After that she disappeared until 1924, when she returned to the family for her brother Arthur's funeral. Although Clara and her surviving brothers and sisters were estranged for many years, they had reconciled by the time I knew them. Clara and her sister Ida lived on the main floor of a large Tudor house in Spokane, and her youngest brother, William, and his wife lived on the top floor. My cousins, sisters, and I looked forward to visits when we could explore the attic and shout important messages into the speaking tube that connected the floors.

In 1950, Aunt Thelma (my father's sister) took me to Sacred Heart Hospital to see Great-Aunt Clara for the last time. Children weren't usually allowed on patient floors in those days, so Aunt Thelma must have convinced the nuns that I was an exceptionally quiet child who absolutely had to see her Great-Aunt Clara again before she died. It's as if my aunt knew that many years later I would want to tell Clara's story and would need a clear memory of her.

Clara is described by other family members as an intelligent, detached observer and a competent businesswoman. She kept her vow never to write about her trip across the country, and as far as I know, she did not publish any writing. She enjoyed writing for her own amusement, though. Several letters she wrote to a niece eighty years ago survive to this day. They are written in verse, sprinkled with fairies and magic.

Helga and Clara inspired me to persevere in my attempts to tell their story even after twenty-nine rejections. I just kept taking classes, writing, and rewriting one word at a time for nearly fifteen years before seeing this book in print. I hope Helga and Clara inspire you, too, to keep on walking in the direction you want to go, one step at a time.

ACKNOWLEDGMENTS

If you picture me writing at a battered desk with nothing but a napping cat for company, you'd be right for ninety-five percent of the time. But it's the other five percent of the time in the real or digital company of editors, teachers, librarians, relatives with stories to tell, other writers, and forthright early readers that is the most important. Here, then, are my five percent people. I'm sorry if I left anyone out—it's been fifteen years since I started the project and my memory is, alas, fallible.

Jennifer Wingertzahn, my acquiring editor at Clarion, who helped me pare 150 pages and find the real story. Dinah Stevenson, publisher at Clarion, who let Jennifer take a chance on me. Daniel Nayeri, who coaxed me into writing a new beginning and fixing the middle and the end. Everyone else at Clarion, including Christine Kettner, Amy Carlisle, and Alison Kerr Miller.

My critique group: Deb Lund, Pamela Greenwood, Penny Holland, and Ruby Tanaka. My favorite teachers: Brenda Guiberson, Janet Lee Carey, Darcy Pattison, and Patricia Lee Gauch. Early readers: my sisters, Rollanda O'Connor and Helen Barr, my daughter, Emily Dagg, and Kaitlin Senter, Bev Katz Rosenbaum, Teresa Gemmer, Kate Snow, and Meg Lippert.

Everyone in the Seattle chapter of the Society of Children's Book Writers and Illustrators. Candy Moonshower, who nominated me for the Sue Alexander Award, and Sue Alexander, who chose an early version of this book to receive the award. Librarians across the country who scrolled through microfilm of local papers to make copies of articles about Clara and Helga.

Preservers of the family legend: Dorothy and Darryl Bahr, Mary K. Irwin, Aunt Thelma and Uncle Harold, Great-Aunt Margaret, and my parents, Wanda and Rolland Estby.

And, of course, Great-Aunt Clara and Great-Grandmother Helga, who lived the story.

Spokane
Washington
Walla Walla
Pendleton
La Grande
Baker City
Oregon
Idaho
Boise
Shoshone
Montana
North Dakota
South Dakota
Wyoming
Rock Springs
Nebraska
Laramie
Cheyenne
North Platte
Lincoln
Nevada
Salt Lake City
Greeley
Denver
Utah
California
Colorado
Kansas
Oklahoma Territory
Arizona Territory
New Mexico Territory
Texas